HER COWBOY
BILLIONAIRE BEST MAN

Christmas in Coral Canyon Romance Book 8

LIZ ISAACSON

AEJ
CREATIVE WORKS

CHAPTER 1

C elia Armstrong ducked out of the kitchen at Whiskey Mountain Lodge, glad this wedding had been scheduled in the winter. Because, wow. This kitchen radiated with heat from all the cooking she'd been doing.

Her hair felt flat and lifeless, and she moved down the hall toward the guest bathroom in Beau and Lily's suite. The lodge seemed stuffed with noise, and it actually warmed Celia's heart. Her house was entirely too quiet these days, and she loved coming up to Whiskey Mountain Lodge and spending time with the Whittakers.

In the bathroom, she spruced up her hair and pulled a tube of lip gloss out of her purse. With perfectly pink and shiny lips, she finally felt ready to attend a wedding. And not just any wedding. Her best friend's wedding.

Amanda Whittaker had been dating for several years, and she'd finally found the perfect cowboy for her. Of course, she'd never really been looking for a cowboy, and Celia hadn't been looking at all.

"You should be," she murmured to her reflection, wondering when her hair had gotten quite so gray. She was fifty-five now, and Brandon had died twenty years ago. Celia had been right in the thick of raising her two daughters, and she hadn't needed anything or anyone else.

There hadn't been *time* for anything or anyone else. With a five-year-old and a one-year-old, Celia had often felt like she was drowning.

But her daughters were both grown now, both in college, and both living somewhere else.

Maybe it's time, she thought, her eyes pressing closed in a long blink. A sense of peace came over her, and she tipped her chin toward the ceiling, imagining her thoughts could get all the way to heaven.

"Dear Lord," she began, the way she had for many years when she had no idea what to do. How to get Reagan's fever down. How to get Ruth to eat something more than chicken nuggets.

"Could I find another husband?" she asked, hoping the Lord would send a direct sign to her eyes and ears.

Of course, He didn't. She'd learned over the years that His plans for her were much more subtle. Sometimes she wondered if He was even there, and then He would remind her in powerful ways that He was.

Someone knocked on the door. "Hey, Celia," Beau said, his voice light and carefree. "Um, there's a problem in the kitchen...."

"What did you boys touch?" she asked, giving him a smile as she stepped past him into the hall.

"Nothing, I swear," he said. "Someone asked for coffee, and I've seen Graham pour coffee before. But the mug cracked, and now there's some sort of problem."

Celia heard the commotion coming from the kitchen, and she wondered what had possessed Amanda to choose the lodge to get married. It was a huge building, sure. Many bedrooms upstairs, a few downstairs, and a theater room. The kitchen and dining room took up a third of the main level, and the master suite took up another third, leaving only a third for a living room where the ceremony would take place in half an hour.

Who needed coffee thirty minutes before a wedding?

She rounded the corner into the kitchen to find Graham and Laney there, each holding a towel. "It's fine," Graham said when he saw her. "We didn't touch the food, and nothing got damaged."

Celia's eyes still swept the trays and trays of appetizers she'd spent many hours prepping. Nothing seemed out of the ordinary, and she finally looked back at Graham.

"Why'd you go get her?" Graham asked Beau, taking off his hat and running his hands through his hair. He wore a tuxedo, and he didn't seem super happy about it. But he'd do anything for his mother, Celia knew that. He threw the coffee-stained towel in the kitchen sink, and Celia moved to get it.

She took the one from Laney too and said, "It's fine, Graham. Is everything ready for the wedding?"

"It better be," Laney said with a grateful smile. "Everything looks great, Celia."

"Thanks. I'm just going to put these in the washing machine." Celia slipped out of the kitchen again, unsure as to why all these people here were causing so much anxiety to trip through her.

She loved having a houseful of people, and she'd thrived on the Christmas Eve meals here for the past eight years. Why she felt so lonely today, she wasn't sure. A sigh leaked from her mouth as she tossed the towels in the washing machine and stayed in the quiet laundry room.

The sound of the back door opening, and a couple of male voices, indicated two men had just come in from outside. One man chuckled. Celia turned and caught a glimpse of him as he moved past the entrance to the laundry room, but he also wore a black jacket across those broad shoulders, black slacks, as well as a charcoal-colored cowboy hat.

Celia had grown up in Wyoming and spent her whole life in the presence of cowboys. They were her kryptonite, and she wondered if the man walking with Finn was single. He'd brought a friend to the wedding, as well as his daughters and their boyfriends.

So maybe....

The man paused in the doorway and turned toward Finn, providing Celia with a nice profile, what with that strong jaw and full lips.

He looked a little bit familiar to her. How that was

possible, she didn't know. She'd lived in Coral Canyon so long, she knew everyone. Of course, so had Amanda, and she'd found a new husband in Dog Valley.

And this guy was talking to Finn. Perhaps he lived in the small town thirty minutes north of Coral Canyon too.

He glanced back the way he'd come, and Celia's heart started bouncing around inside her chest. He was extremely handsome, and a smile touched his mouth as he followed Finn and left Celia's eyesight.

Alone, she pressed one palm to her pulse, almost willing it to calm down.

She was definitely ready to start dating again, and she thought, *Thank You, Lord*, before heading down the hall after that handsome cowboy toward the living room. After all, her best friend was about to get married.

Before she could take too many steps, really get a good look at that cowboy who'd accelerated her pulse with a chuckle and a smile, someone called her name. A fair bit of panic rode in the two syllables, and she hurried back into the kitchen to find Stockton standing in the middle of a couple dozen tarts.

Eli's face looked like he'd been stung by an army of red ants. His face shone with anger, the bright red so not like him. "Stockton," he barked. "I told you not to come in here."

"It's fine," Celia said, though she had no time to make more tarts. It was fine. They could make everything work with less.

"I'll pick them up," Stockton said, his voice high-pitched and tinny. The boy had just turned eleven, and he and his parents and sister had just moved back to Coral Canyon three weeks ago. He stooped, his perfectly polished shoe squishing a cherry tart.

"Stockton." Eli sounded one breath away from losing it completely.

Celia looked at him and stepped between him and the child and said, "Eli, it was an accident. I'll take him to clean up. Could you get these in the trashcan, please?"

His face crumbled. "Celia—"

"It's fine." She glanced over as Beau appeared in the doorway. "Beau will help you." She pointed to the floor. "Clean this up. Your mother doesn't need to know."

Beau's jaw clenched, and he nodded. Celia turned, put her arm around Stockton, and said, "Take off your shoe, Stocky."

He did, and Celia took it. "This will clean up easily." She wished all the windows were open, as she felt so dang hot. "Come on, baby," she said, and Stockton swiped at his face as he spun and marched out of the kitchen, his gait uneven with only one polished, black shoe on his feet.

She followed him back to the bathroom where she'd freshened up. She felt like no amount of lip gloss could conceal how harried and stressed she was.

"I'm sorry, Celia," Stockton said, his tears still brimming in those innocent eyes.

"It's fine," she said. "They're tarts. No big deal." She glanced at him as she bent to get a washcloth out of the vanity. "Did your dad tell you to stay out of the kitchen?"

"Yeah." Stockton looked miserable. "But me and Bailey just wanted to run down to the barn real quick."

"Your grandmother is getting married in ten minutes. You thought you had time to get down to the barn real quick?" She turned on the water and smiled at the boy. "I miss you, bud." She gathered him into a hug, suddenly anxious for her own grandchildren. "I'm glad you've moved back here."

"Will you make those apple ebelskivers sometime?" he asked, sniffling as he cried into her chest. Celia's heart expanded with love for this boy, and he didn't even belong to her by blood. But he definitely belonged to her in some way.

"Tomorrow if you want," she said, stepping back and brushing the tears from his face. "Now, let's get this pie off your shoe. Your grandma won't like that in her wedding party."

Stockton stood and watched her clean it up, telling her about his school project. She got his shoe back on, and she hugged him again. "You should apologize to your dad."

"I know. I will." Stockton squeezed her tight and then left the bathroom. She sighed, one more trip to the laundry room in her future.

She caught sight of that charcoal-colored hat as she passed the living room entrance, and somehow, the cowboy felt the weight of her gaze, and their eyes met again. Something familiar struck her in the chest. She knew him....

"Time to line up," someone said, and Celia increased

her pace. Even though it only took a few seconds to get the cherry pie washcloth in the washing machine, by the time she returned to the hallway, it seemed everyone had a partner.

Except her.

Her breath caught in her throat, and she felt at a loss for what to do. This was a familiar feeling for Celia, as the moment Brandon had died, she'd been adrift with two small children. Everything became *except her*. Everyone had someone to sit by at church—except her. Everyone had a date on Valentine's Day—except her. Everyone had someone to watch their children for ladies night at the rec center—except her.

She'd had to figure things out as she went. Find babysitters. Sit by the pastor's wife. Make cakes and bacon bouquets for her and Reagan and Ruth on Valentine's Day.

As if Moses himself had arrived to part the Red Sea, the crowd shifted, showing her the cowboy in the charcoal-colored hat.

"Need a partner?" he asked, that delicious smile on his face. He took a couple steps past Beau and Lily, and a horrible realization hit her with the force of a ton of bricks.

She did know him.

Zach Zuckerman.

She sucked in a breath, the memories from her childhood rushing through her like river rapids.

"Zach," she hissed, an undeniable and inexplicable fury and dislike overcoming her.

He paused, cocked his head, and studied her. Not three seconds passed before he said, "Celia Abbott." His smile vanished, and he looked at her with the same disdain all Abbotts had for the Zuckermans.

Going back for as many generations as Celia could remember, the Abbotts and Zuckermans had been enemies. They still owned ranches across the road from one another in Coral Canyon, and the feud continued to this day.

Celia didn't even remember what it was about.

But she knew she couldn't date Zach Zuckerman. Period. The end.

"Go on," Graham said, nudging Zach to the front of the line. "You're the best man, Zach. Celia, you're with him. It's time to start."

Celia looked at Zach, wondering how in the world this had happened. How he'd gotten here, inside the lodge that had become a sanctuary for her. How she could possibly link her arm through his and smile, even for a moment. Even for Amanda.

"Celia," Graham hissed, and she realized Zach had moved and had his elbow cocked toward her.

Seeing no other choice, she put her arm in his and faced the front.

CHAPTER 2

Zach Zuckerman couldn't believe his rotten luck. The first woman to catch his eye in a couple of years, and she was an Abbott.

He wanted to shake his fist at heaven and ask, "Really, Lord?"

But he should probably shake his fist toward the ground and say, "Not today, Satan. Not today."

No matter what, he was going to walk down the aisle with an Abbott on his arm. Of course, she wasn't an Abbott anymore. She'd grown up and gotten married, same as him. Her husband had been his best friend in high school, and Brandon had died a number of years ago. There was nothing his grandfather had liked to do more than trash-talk the Abbotts, but even he'd been reverent when the news came of Brandon Armstrong's death.

A couple of years later, Gramps had passed himself. Zach was glad he hadn't been alive when Zach's own marriage had fallen apart. When Kathy had filed for divorce and taken the kids to Boise.

Twelve years later, Zach still lived on the farm in Dog Valley where he'd envisioned he and Kathy growing old together. He'd always found comfort in his friendship with Finn, as the man seemed perfectly happy alone on his farm on the other side of town.

But now his best friend had gone and found himself someone to share his life with in a way that Zach desperately wanted for himself.

And until five minutes ago, he'd been thinking maybe something good would come out of his long drive on snow-packed roads and him dressing in his nicest suit.

A date with a pretty woman.

Too bad he hadn't recognized her sooner.

He tried not to breathe in the fruity, flowery scent of the woman next to him. Tried not to notice the way her arm fit in his. Tried not to focus more on her than on the ceremony in front of him.

He failed at all three, and all he could do was pray the wedding would conclude quickly so he could get a lungful of air that didn't tantalize him.

Why? ran through his mind. Why had God allowed her to come *back* into his life? *Why? Why? Why?*

The word practically screamed through his mind, and he turned away from her slightly and took a deep breath.

Even if she wasn't an Abbott, Zach still wouldn't have pursued her. Brandon had always been like a brother to him, and he had no desire to dig up old memories with the man's widow. Surely she wouldn't want that either.

He finally managed to pull himself from his own mind and focus on the best friend he had now. Finn glowed with happiness as the ceremony concluded and he kissed his new wife. Zach clapped and cheered along with everyone else, a rush of joy painting over the stress he normally dealt with behind closed doors and gates.

Celia stepped away from him, clapping same as him. She wore a beautiful smile to go with that flattering blue dress—the one that had caught Zach's eye at least an hour ago. Amanda's sons filled the lodge with whistling, and Zach couldn't help laughing.

He also couldn't help thinking of his own children, his own family. He was the second oldest of four boys, and he'd been secretly glad he hadn't had to decide if he'd stay on the family farm or not.

The feud between the Abbotts and the Zuckermans bothered Kathy, and she hadn't wanted Zach to be part of it. They'd chosen a quiet life in Dog Valley—until that became *too* quiet for her.

Zach had never even considered returning to Coral Canyon or the family farm. That place had a spirit all its own, and it could poison a man's heart.

It had, actually. Many times.

His oldest brother, Owen, ran the place now, and he spewed as much vitriol about the Abbott's as most of the other Zuckerman's. Another glance at Celia found her watching him too, and their eyes locked.

He felt the smile slipping from his face no matter how hard he tried to hold onto it. He could not imagine a reality where he drove down that winding dirt road to the house where he'd grown up, opened the door for her, and took her inside to meet Owen.

No way he could ever do that.

Ever.

She managed to smile at him, duck her pretty head, and turn toward the kitchen. He felt like a satellite, like he needed to be stay near her, orbit around her. Her spirit called to his soul, and he found himself following her.

Thankfully, so did everyone else, as the next stage of the wedding would obviously take place in the kitchen.

In fact, Celia seemed to be in charge, as everyone turned toward her as she spoke in a loud voice. "Congratulations to the bride and groom!"

Another cheer went up before she got down to business. "Now we have all of Finn and Amanda's favorites here. Cherry pie. That's for you, Finn." She beamed at the man with affection on her face, and Zach wondered what that would feel like.

It had been entirely too long since he'd had the gentle touch, the soft influence, of a woman in his life.

And suddenly, his family didn't matter. If he wanted to go out with Celia Armstrong, he could. Should, in fact, if the way his heartbeat raced told him anything. He thought of his daughter and what Lindsey might say if she found out he was seeing someone.

"About time, Dad."

The words looped in his mind as he listened to Celia detail the chocolate mousse cake, and then pull out a tray of chicken salad croissants and say, "Amanda makes these for every family party she has. It seemed only fitting we'd have them at her wedding."

The two women embraced, and chaos erupted as people started grabbing plates and napkins and helping their kids through the line.

Zach stood back, watching. He didn't have any grandchildren yet, but Finn absolutely shone as he took a baby from someone.

To his great surprise, he found himself standing next to Celia only a few moments later. "Did you make all the food?" he asked, though it was obvious she did.

"Yes," she said, keeping her eyes on the family in front of them. By his count, Finn had invited just him, his daughters and their boyfriends, and his parents. Zach knew the man was private, and he wondered who in the world he'd invite to a second wedding.

Certainly not the horde of people he and Kathy had hosted at their ceremony. And if Celia was the one across the altar....

Zach shook his head, because the idea was so ridiculous. So far-fetched. He hadn't spoken to an Abbott since third grade when he'd screamed at her oldest brother Mack to leave Owen alone.

He hadn't known that it was Owen who'd started the fight on the school bus. He honestly didn't know which family had started the feud, but he knew it was over some land that bordered their properties, as well as the water rights that flowed from the Abbott's side of the street to the Zuckerman's land on the south.

As far as he knew, her two older brothers ran the Abbott place together, but he hadn't kept up with the town gossip in Coral Canyon for at least three decades. Probably longer, as rumors and who was dating whom had never appealed to Zach.

"It looks delicious," he said.

"I work for the Whittakers," she said, finally looking at him. She possessed a pair of sparkling hazel eyes that harbored so many unsaid words. Zach couldn't seem to look away as she continued with, "I'm their personal chef here at the lodge. I come up and cook a few times a week."

"That's great," fell from his mouth, but he didn't remember his brain instructing his vocal cords to speak.

She nodded like she'd done her duty by talking to him for sixty seconds. "What do you do?" she asked at the same time he said, "What do you do on the other days?"

She blinked, surprise moving through those lovely eyes. "I used to have several private chef jobs," she said. "But I gave them all up when Graham hired me. He pays really well."

"Seems like he's doing well," Zach said, glancing around the lodge.

Celia started to say something, but a crash in the kitchen had her jumping and then hurrying away from him. Zach would usually leave at this point. The chicken salad croissants looked amazing, sure. But he knew where to get a good hamburger in town, and it was supposed to snow again this afternoon.

Yet he didn't leave. He leaned against the wall and pushed his cowboy hat lower over his eyes, until he could just barely see Celia as she helped clean up the mess a small girl had made.

"Stop staring and come eat," Finn said, stepping between him and Celia, effectively ruining Zach's line of sight.

"I'm not staring," he said quickly.

"Of course you are." Finn grinned at him. "I've seen the push-your-hat-down thing before, Zach. She's pretty. You going to get her number?"

Yes, Zach thought at the same time he shook his head no.

"Why not? Still not dating?"

"Not her," Zach said.

Finn's eyebrows crinkled in confusion, and Zach pushed away from the wall, unwilling to say much more.

"Amanda and I are leaving on our honeymoon in the morning," Finn said. "If you want her number, you're going to have to get it yourself while you're here, or text me pretty quick." Finn turned and went back toward the kitchen.

Zach went with him, because he didn't need to cause a scene at his best friend's wedding. As he loaded a small party plate with a croissant, some mousse cake, and two of the peach pie tartlets, he couldn't help imagining what it would be like to go out with Celia.

No one else had to know. She might not even like him. He might not be able to tolerate her. Perhaps the blood between all Abbotts and all Zuckermans would be bad.

And so he found himself loitering near her in the kitchen instead of going into the dining room to eat. "If a man wanted to get your number, what would he have to do?" He shoved a whole peach tartlet in his mouth, so he'd have time to think before he said anything else.

Celia whipped her head toward him, the panic and shock in her face speaking of the generations of loathing between them. "Are you serious?"

He swallowed, going over all the reasons he should walk away now. Keep his head high and get the heck out of there. Stat. But Brandon had been gone for a long time. And he would have to figure out how to deal with the feud between their families.

"I think so," he said. "One date. If it's too hard, or it doesn't work out, fine. We walk away. No big deal."

Celia huffed and returned her attention to the scene before them. Zach could practically hear the wheels turning in her head, and he liked it. She was considering it —that meant something. It meant she'd liked what she'd seen of him before she recognized him, same as he had for her.

He finished all the food on his plate, and she still hadn't said a single digit. Folding the plate in half, he said, "Well, I have animals to care for this afternoon. Double duty, actually, as I'm handling Finn's farm while he and Amanda are gone." He tipped his hat at her and stepped in front of her to throw his trash in the huge can in front of the oven.

"Give me your number," she whispered when he was right in front of her. He paused and looked down at her. Only a couple of inches separated their bodies, and he instantly felt hot all over.

"Yeah?" he asked, his voice almost as quiet as hers had been.

A flush climbed into her cheeks, and she twisted and picked up a pen. "Hurry, or someone will notice."

"And you don't want that." Zach didn't phrase it as a question. These people were practically Celia's family, and he quickly rattled off his phone number while she scrawled it on a piece of paper. She ripped that from the notebook, balled up the paper, and opened the top drawer where he'd been standing. She put the wadded-up paper in there and looked at him.

"I'm the only one who'll even notice that." She flashed him that smile again, and Zach's whole being lit up.

"All right, then," he said. "I'm a farmer, Celia. Call early, but don't call late." With that, he touched the brim of his hat, threw his plate away, and escaped the kitchen.

CHAPTER 3

After the wedding, Celia didn't go back up to Whiskey Mountain Lodge for a few days. Number one, Mother Nature had dumped a foot of snow overnight, and not many people were going anywhere around Coral Canyon.

Of course, Amanda had noticed the way Zach had stood by Celia as he ate, and she'd asked a few questions. Celia had managed to learn more from Amanda than she gave away, and she knew Zach lived in Dog Valley, same as Finn.

"Same as Amanda, once she gets back," Celia reminded herself as she opened the door to the cabinet where she kept her yarn. She wasn't feeling particularly creative that morning, and she didn't have any grandchildren to knit little sweaters for.

She did, however, have a little dog who definitely

needed another sweater before he outgrew the last one she'd made him.

A familiar pang of sadness hit her when she looked down at the snoozing black Lab at her feet. She'd just gotten him a couple of months ago in honor of Bear, the black Lab Graham had inherited when his father had passed away.

Well, now Bear had gone all the way of the Earth, and Celia couldn't bear her time at the lodge without the old black Lab. So she'd gotten Grizz, a new black Lab, to accompany her during her hours at the lodge.

And at home, as he never ventured far from her side. Getting a puppy in the middle of the Wyoming winter had been challenging, to say the least, but Celia had survived the midnight potty training, and now Grizz just needed something to keep his chewing urges satisfied, a good spot next to her while she knitted, and his puppy chow.

When the weather warmed up, she'd teach him how to walk on a leash, how to chase a ball, and how to round up the few horses and cows up at the lodge. Maybe. Celia didn't actually know how to train a dog, but she sure did like the company of one.

"What color, Grizz?" she asked, but he just lifted his head and looked at her. "Be that way. I think green."

Celia glanced at the crumpled paper on the end table as she sat down. Grizz jumped up on the couch beside her and leaned into her side before settling into her thigh.

Zach's number.

She still hadn't called him.

She wasn't sure why she'd even agreed to take his number in the first place. His question about what it would take to get her number was made of sheer insanity. He knew exactly who she was, and she hadn't been able to get rid of Brandon's words about his once-best-friend.

He's a good man, Brandon had told her countless times.

She'd lost the sound of her husband's voice many years ago, but she could still picture him. Still smell the after-shave he used before heading out the back door to the fields, the barns, the cattle, the goats, the life of a farmer.

Celia hadn't kept up the farm after his death, but she hadn't been able to part with it either. She sold all the animals and simply lived in the house Brandon had promised he'd fix up for her.

He'd tried, but the workload around the farm was too much for one man, and they didn't have the funds to hire help as their family was young and growing. And once the cancer treatments started....

Celia pushed the thoughts from her mind. They didn't bring sadness or bitterness anymore, though both of those emotions had spent plenty of time in Celia's company. Now, though, she simply missed him. Missed the life she was supposed to have with him.

Missed the rough yet gentle touch of a man's hand against her cheek as he kissed her hello after a day spent under the hot summer sun. Missed the way male laughter could fill a house as he told jokes to his daughters. Missed the scent of leather, and land, and lumber that seemed to permeate the very air around a man.

A sigh slipped from her lips as she started the sweater Grizz would wear as soon as he grew for a few more weeks.

So why don't you want to call Zach? she asked herself, her fingers and needles practically clashing as they moved.

If she did, she'd be admitting she wanted to go out with him, and that felt like a very big step for Celia. It *was* a very big step.

Her phone rang, startling her and causing her to drop one of her needles. Grizz barked, and she said, "Hush. It's the phone." She reached for it, her heart hammering as if the big, broad cowboy was calling her.

But of course, he couldn't be. He didn't have her number.

"Reagan," she said after she answered. "How are you, sweetie?"

"Hey, Momma. How's Grizz?"

Celia paused, her head automatically cocking as she heard the buzz in her daughter's voice. "What's going on?"

"Nothing," she said, but Reagan's voice carried amusement. She was probably about to shriek, and Celia held the phone away from her ear.

Sure enough, in the next moment, the shrill noise came through the line. "Mom, Dale asked me to marry him!"

Happiness rushed through Celia. No, joy. "Praise the

Lord," she said, bringing the phone back to her mouth. "Tell me about it."

Of course Reagan was going to tell her about it. That was why her daughter had called in the middle of the day on a Friday. Celia loved listening to the excitement in her daughter's voice, and she loved Dale too. They two of them had been dating for two years, and they were both set to graduate from the University of Wyoming in just a few months.

"So what are you thinking for a date?" Celia asked, setting aside her knitting in favor of her planner. Yes, it was still on paper, though both of her daughters had tried to get her to convert to an app. An online calendar. Something. They'd even created one they could share, but she only looked at their events; she never created any of her own.

What would she put on it? *Knitting, 8 am to noon.*

No, thank you.

"We're going to wait and see what jobs Dale might get," she said. "The interviews for the engineering graduates start next week. Then we'll decide. If he gets a job out-of-state, I'll want to get married before we go in the fall. But if not, I'd kind of like a Christmas wedding."

"That's less than a year, either way," Celia said, flipping ahead to September as if she had any conflicts written on the calendar.

"We can do it, Momma," Reagan said. "I'm not fussy, remember? That's Ruth."

"Ah." Celia smiled, because Reagan was more of a

throw-her-hair-in-a-ponytail type of girl while Ruth curled every strand into ringlets. "Well, I'm open. I didn't like the winter wedding, but if that's what you want."

"How was Amanda's wedding?"

Celia looked up from her planner, her thoughts automatically moving to the best man at the wedding. "It was lovely," she said. "She and Finn are so happy."

Reagan didn't ask if Celia had met anyone, though she and Dale had met at a wedding. Reagan had stopped talking about Celia dating about five years ago, and Celia had been glad at the time. Now, though, she wanted her daughter to ask her. Maybe she could work through some of the things troubling her if she could talk about them with someone.

"I have another question," Celia said.

"I'm coming home for Spring Break, so we can plan everything," Reagan said. "That's only three weeks away."

Celia cleared her throat. "All right. This is…about me."

Reagan said nothing, and Celia wondered if she'd shocked her daughter into silence. Determined not to chicken out, she blurted, "I met a man."

More silence, and Celia could not predict what Reagan was thinking or what she'd do. So when another shriek came through the line, Celia took the full brunt of it right in her eardrum.

"Momma!" Reagan rushed on to ask about six questions in the span of one breath, and Celia started laughing too.

"Slow down, honey. He was a guest at the wedding.

The best man, actually." Celia didn't know what else to say. She'd never been too terribly affected by the feud between her family and Zach's, as her brothers had inherited the farm. She'd left for college, met Brandon—though he was a Coral Canyon native too—and gotten married. They'd had twelve wonderful years together before the Lord had called him home.

Celia shook her head, her ability to speak somewhere behind the lump in her throat.

"Are you going to go out with him?" Reagan asked.

"I don't know," Celia managed to say through the tightness at the back of her tongue.

"Momma," Reagan said, sobering. "You should. Tell me what you're doing right now. Wait." Her voice snapped, and Celia knew what was coming. She reached over and patted Grizz.

"You're knitting. *Knitting*, mother, when you could be getting ready for a fun lunch with a man."

"You don't even know who it is."

"It doesn't matter, Mom. You should go out with him. You haven't gone out with anyone since Daddy died. No one. Not one single person. Not even coffee, or—"

"Okay, Reagan," Celia said. She didn't want to argue with her daughter. Her eyes landed on the notebook paper again, and she said, "I think I'll call him."

Reagan squealed, and she said, "I'm calling Ruthie right now. Call me back as soon as you can." The line went dead, and Celia chuckled as she lowered the phone to her lap. She didn't need the paper, as she'd programmed Zach's number into her phone days ago.

Feeling reckless and brave at the same time, she swiped and tapped to bring up his contact. With trembling fingers, she finally touched the green call button and lifted the device to her ear.

CHAPTER 4

Zach didn't answer calls from numbers he didn't know. He found them annoying, and the last couple he'd answered had tried to get him to sign up for some bogus life insurance policy he didn't need.

Maybe he was in a bad mood, because five full days had passed since he'd given Celia Armstrong his number. The woman hadn't even so much as texted him a simple hello.

"Celia," he said, spinning back toward the shelf where he housed his phone while he worked in the barn. What if that phone call had been her? And he hadn't answered.

He held very still for some reason, wishing there was a way to determine who'd called. He yearned for the simpler times of his youth, where there was a way to figure out who'd called with a reverse look-up feature. Such a thing only existed on landlines now, and he couldn't remember the last time he'd had one of those.

Lindsey had said exactly what Zach had predicted she would, and he'd resorted to praying for the Lord to influence Celia enough to call him.

His more level-headed daughter, Abby, had texted every day, asking if he had a date with the woman he'd met at the wedding yet. Could he tell her later today that he did?

He strode over to the shelf and grabbed his phone. The number had a Wyoming area code, and his heart started tippity-tapping in his chest. No voicemail icon came up. Zach hesitated, his thoughts flinging themselves around inside his mind so quickly, he couldn't grab onto one and make sense of it.

Tapping quickly, he sent a message to Abby. *I think that woman may have called, and I missed it. Do I call her back?*

He enjoyed the texting relationship he had with Abby. If he'd sent the same message to Lindsey, she'd call him. But Abby was deaf and couldn't really talk on the phone much at all. So everything was a text, and giant letters appeared on the screen in the next moment.

DAD – YES CALL HER BACK RIGHT NOW.

Relief surged through Zach, and his fingers seemed to have brains of their own as they tapped and swiped and lifted the phone to his ear.

"Hello, Zach," Celia's cool voice said, and he had nothing to respond with. She made his heart sing with two simple words, and he simply enjoyed the vibrations of that music in his soul.

"Are you there?" she asked, a hint of confusion in her tone now.

"Yeah," he blurted. "Yes. Yes, I'm here." He cleared his throat, cursing himself for every sound he'd just made. All of them painted him as nervous, and he didn't want her to know she made him nervous.

But oh, she did. Just the idea of going out with her had his pulse jackhammering in his chest, the same way it had when he'd sold his last parcel of real estate to a huge conglomerate for over three billion dollars.

"I was wondering what you're doing for lunch today," Celia asked. "The weather's cleared up a little, and I think I could stand to leave the house today."

Zach chuckled. "It's been terrible, hasn't it?" Of course, he still had to get out on the farm and get the chores done, but maybe she'd held off on calling him because she didn't want to drive in the snow.

"I'm not sure why I still live here, to be honest." Celia laughed, the high, twinkling sound making Zach's blood heat even further.

"I'm free for lunch," Zach said. He had no idea what he'd been doing when his phone rang, nor what chores he had left. But he knew he could get away for a couple of hours to eat with Celia. "Do you have a favorite spot?"

"I was thinking I'd come up there," she said. "You live in Dog Valley, right?"

"That's right," he said, his mind zipping down the

quaint Main Street in town. "There's a pretty great diner here. They have a good salad bar on Fridays."

"I do like a good salad bar…how did you know that?"

"Lucky guess," he said with a smile. He couldn't believe he was talking to a woman. And not any woman. Celia Abbot. Armstrong. Whatever. He remembered those beautiful eyes, and the way she took care of everyone and everything at the lodge.

Maybe she needed someone to take care of her.

"I can come pick you up," he said. "Then you don't have to drive."

"Oh, that's unnecessary," she said. "You'd be in the car for hours today if you did that."

"I don't mind," he said, hoping that didn't give away how badly he wanted to see her again. Which was absolutely crazy.

"Is it the Dog Valley Diner?"

"Yeah," he said with a chuckle, moving toward the loft in the barn. "We're not great with creative names up here. Sometimes people call it the DVD."

"DVD," she repeated. "Like a movie."

"I guess." He cursed himself for this lame conversation. Someone his age should know how to talk to a woman by now, but he reminded himself that he'd lived alone for over fifteen years, and dogs didn't care if he lacked wit.

"Noon?" she asked.

"Sure," he said. "They'll be hopping at noon, but we shouldn't have to wait long."

"Great," she said. "I'll see you then." She carried a smile in her voice, and dang if Zach didn't have a grin splitting his whole face.

"See you then," he repeated, and they said good-bye. He let his hand holding the phone drop to his side, a sigh filling his whole chest before leaking out.

He turned in a full circle, as if just now realizing he stood in the barn. What had he been doing in here?

A few seconds passed before he remembered. "Hay," he said out loud. "Get the cows fed. Get in the shower."

With a new plan in mind, he got back to work, Celia never far from his thoughts.

☙❧

NOON ARRIVED, and with it Zach walked through the front door of the diner. A wall of noise met his ears, but the sight of Celia rising from the bench made everything silent again.

"Hey," he said, his voice a bit breathless for reasons he couldn't name. "I feel bad you had to drive all the way up here. Next time, let me come down to Coral Canyon."

"Next time?" Celia's eyebrows went up. "I seem to recall you saying we could walk away after this."

Paralyzing fear struck Zach right behind the ribs. "Well, sure," he somehow managed to say. "If we don't think it'll work out."

"I don't see how we could possibly know after one date if *everything* will work out." She gave him a dazzling—flirtatious?—smile and stepped over to the hostess stand. "He's here."

"I'm ready for you then," the woman there said. She glanced back to Zach, obviously recognizing him. "Hey. Right this way."

Thankfully, Starla didn't say anything else. Not that Zach had anything to be ashamed of. She placed menus on the table with, "Your server will be right over," and Zach took a moment to settle himself on one side of the booth.

Celia took longer than that, and when she finally looked up at him, she wore all kinds of emotions in her gaze. Apprehension was the biggest one, and Zach wanted to wipe it right off her face.

"I want to just get something out there," she said, folding her arms on the table as if this were a super-fancy restaurant.

"All right." He glanced around for an anchor, something to hold while she confessed. A glass of water would've done nicely, but they had nothing.

"I haven't dated since Brandon died."

"Oh." Zach blinked, dozens of memories assaulting him at the same time new emotions surged through him. "I'm so sorry about Brandon."

Celia nodded. "He's been gone a very long time."

"Twenty years," Zach said. "You've never gone out with anyone since?"

"You'd be the first."

The pressure along Zach's shoulders increased. "So you have a very high standard." No way he'd meet it. He already had three strikes against him because of his last name. A second date with Celia felt impossible, and in fact, Zach wondered if he should get up and leave the diner now.

"I have no standard," Celia said. "I just...I'm nervous, that's all." She swallowed, and Zach tracked the movement of her throat.

"My wife and I got divorced fifteen years ago," he said. "I haven't dated much since."

"But you have dated," she said.

"I went out with one woman, one time," he said with a shrug. "If that counts as 'dated,' then I suppose I have."

She nodded, glancing up when a waiter arrived with two glasses of water. Zach coached himself not to dive for his, but he reached for the straw very slowly.

"We haven't even looked at the menu," Zach said to the waiter, a man he knew pretty well, actually.

Harry smiled at them. "Take your time. I'll circle back." He left, and Zach picked up the menu to at least pretend like he could read in the presence of this pretty woman.

"What's good here?" she asked, looking at her menu too.

"Everything," he said. "Are you going to go for the salad bar?"

"Probably," she said. "And the BLT." She put her menu down and met his gaze again, something new storming in hers already.

"What?" he asked.

"Brandon always said you were a good man."

Zach's throat narrowed, and he nodded. "He was too."

"I don't want to spend our time talking about him."

"All right." Zach focused on the menu again, trying to figure out what he wanted. The woman across from him. Everything. He needed all of life's secrets right now, so he could know what to do, how to act, what to say to keep Celia at his side. Or across from him on dozens of dates.

The fact that his feelings for her were already that strong confused him further, and he wrinkled his eyebrows at the menu.

"Made a choice?" Harry asked, and Celia started rattling off what she wanted.

Zach had no idea. "Bacon cheeseburger and fries," he finally said.

Harry collected the menus and said, "You can go to the salad bar anytime. Plates are over there."

Celia flashed the trademark smile at him and followed the waiter, leaving Zach alone in the booth. He drew in a deep breath, hoping the extra oxygen would clear his head enough to continue this date—and get a second one.

She returned faster than he thought possible, and as she slid into the booth with a plate piled high with lettuce and all the salad toppings the bar held, she asked, "So, Zach. You look like you might have a confession for me too."

"Do I?" He chuckled, sorting through the many things he could tell her. He'd already told her his pathetic dating history. They'd surely spend loads of time talking about their children.

"The only thing I can think of is that I used to be a real estate developer, but I started selling off the land I've had for decades when the market grew hot."

"Ah." She nodded, forking her salad around to get the dressing on everything evenly. "So you're the reason we've got all this growth in the valley." Her hazel eyes sparkled with mischief.

"Probably." He grinned back at her. "I have plenty of money, and I run a very small farm here in town now. It's a very boring life."

"So your confession is that you're boring?"

He shrugged again, liking this game they were playing. "And rich. Bored and rich. It can be a very dangerous combination sometimes."

She laughed, and the sound of it filled Zach's whole soul with joy. He just had to get a second date with her, but the twittering voice in the back of his head jabbering on about Owen and the rest of his family wouldn't go away.

CHAPTER 5

Celia wished Zach wasn't quite so charming. Quite so dashing and dreamy. From his deep voice to that dazzling smile, he was checking boxes for her left and right. And up and down.

"So you returned to farming," she said. "Why didn't you go back to your family's farm?"

"Owen has a family of his own," Zach said, as if that summed everything up. Maybe it did.

"And you?" she asked. "Do you have children?"

"Yes," he said, his face taking on a glow now that Celia could appreciate. He obviously loved his kids, and he hadn't spoken about them yet. "Two daughters and a son. Lindsey is the oldest. She just got accepted to medical school at the University of Washington. She'll probably go there, but she's waiting on something...maybe another school? I need to ask her."

Celia almost felt stupid for eating while he didn't have anything, but before she knew it, their food arrived too. He picked up the ketchup bottle and said, "Abby's at the school for the deaf in Washington, D.C. She's a junior there."

Celia's eyebrows mirrored her surprise, but Zach continued as if he hadn't seen her reaction to finding out he had a deaf daughter.

"And my son is nineteen. Just finished high school last year, and he's still in Boise with his mother." He flashed her a smile then and picked up his hamburger. "You? Children? I think you and Brandon had two daughters."

"Yes," she said. "Just the two. Reagan just got engaged, actually. She and her fiancé are both graduating in the spring. And Ruth is a sophomore at the University of Wyoming too." A flash of pride moved through Celia.

"You sound proud of them," he said.

"I am." Celia sipped her water. "They're good girls." She missed them terribly, but she wasn't going to say that on this date. Probably not even the next one.

The next one.

In that moment, she realized she wanted there to be another date, and then another one. "I have another confession," she said.

"Oh, boy." He dunked a French fry in ketchup and ate it. Fire sparkled in his eyes, and Celia hadn't been out with anyone else in a while, but she could recognize attraction when she saw it. At least she hoped she could.

"I wanted to come up here so no one in Coral Canyon would see us."

Darkness entered Zach's already dark brown eyes. "Is that so?"

"I just...my family doesn't like your family. We should probably talk about that at some point."

"I'm not interested in the feud between our families," he said.

"That doesn't mean it doesn't exist," Celia said, hoping she wasn't about to ruin everything with him. Not that there was much to ruin. A blip of excitement at the wedding. Five days of nerves over calling him. And twenty minutes at lunch so far.

"How close are you to your brothers?"

"Close enough to see them at holidays and sometimes during the week. On my mother's birthday, Mother's Day...." The list could go on, but Celia let her voice die. "I don't think this is something we just ignore, Zach."

Saying his name felt intimate, and Celia liked how easily it moved across her vocal cords.

"I suppose not," he said. "We moved up here to get away from my family."

"You and your wife?"

"Yes, the drama wore on her. On me too." The weariness rode right in his voice.

Celia wondered if maybe the solution could be so simple. "How often do you see your brothers?"

"Often enough that I can't hide a relationship for very long."

So this wasn't going to be simple. Celia should've known that from the start. She did. She nodded and let the conversation move on. Zach told her about his small farm, and she asked him about Abby, and the conversation was easy and light.

"This was so fun," Celia said with absolute truth in her soul. She squinted into the sun as she looked up at Zach.

He adjusted his cowboy hat to hide more of his face. "I had a good time too." His hand landed on her lower back as he guided her down the sidewalk. "What did you think? Maybe we could do something like this again?"

"Well, I want the record to show that I don't have *everything* worked out. I don't know if it will work."

"All right," he said with a grin. "You're going to tease me about that forever."

"Probably." She couldn't help the joyful smile on her face. "And I'd love to go out with you again." She slowed as she approached her car, almost wanting to prolong her time with him. "This is me."

He paused and put one hand on the roof of the sedan. "In Coral Canyon? Or up here?"

"I don't—"

"Because I'm fifty years old," he said. "I'm not sure how old you are, but I remember you being older than Brandon. And I think maybe we should get to make our own decisions."

Celia knew that sounded nice in theory. Looked good on paper. But the fact was, her decisions did impact other people, whether she wanted them to or not.

She felt torn right down the middle. Mack and Lennox would not be impressed with her choice of dates. After all this time, and all the men she could choose from.... They would definitely be upset.

"Maybe I should talk to my brothers," she said.

"And maybe we should just do what we want and deal with them if we have to."

"So you're not going to tell Owen," she said, not making it a question. "Or...I can't remember your other brother's names. Xander?"

"And Gene," he said. "And no, I don't think so." He leaned closer, a flirtatious smile sitting right on that strong mouth now. "But you should know I've told my daughters about you, and they'll probably want all the gory details of our lunch."

Celia tipped her head back and laughed, thrilled when Zach joined his voice to hers. "Good to know," she said. "And I told mine about you. So I'll leave you to text them."

"Oh, Lindsey will call," Zach said. "I think the Good Lord knew I couldn't handle two daughters who wanted to talk everything to death. So Abby'll just text." He beamed at her, and Celia's heart raced with emotion for this man.

"Does she speak at all?"

"A little," he said. "Yeah. She'll want to video chat me so we can talk."

"So you know sign language."

"Yes, ma'am." He put up two fingers on his right hand and moved them in front of his eyes. He pulled them away and said, "See you later." His fingers moved into an

43

L-shape, and he pointed them straight out in front of him.

Foolishness hit Celia full-on behind the ribs. Of course he knew sign language. How else had he communicated with his daughter while she grew up?

"Bye," she said, wanting to repeat the sign to him, but feeling too self-conscious. She slipped into her car while he walked away, a loud sigh leaking from between her lips. "Thank you, Lord."

The whisper of gratitude grew in her heart until a smile had covered her face. As far as first dates went, that one wasn't so bad. Not so bad at all.

❦

THE WEEKEND PASSED, and Celia sat in church with a row of friends. Amanda still wasn't back from her honeymoon, and Celia hadn't found the courage to start texting Zach. She'd told Reagan and Ruth about him, and they both seemed plenty happy that she was seeing someone again.

But did going to lunch with him one time count as "seeing" him? She wasn't sure, and he hadn't texted her either. They hadn't set anything else up.

She saw people in a new light, though, and when Dwight Rogers smiled at her on her way out of church, her heart fluttered. Maybe she should go out with him. He was more business than cowboy, and he worked at the energy company Graham and Andrew ran. He was pretty high up too, if Celia remembered right.

She'd just reached the door when she'd decided to go back and talk to him. The church hosted a linger longer after the sermon, and while she usually didn't stay, maybe today she should.

Her phone rang at that moment, and Zach's name sat on the screen. "Hey," she said, turning away from Dwight completely now. A smile touched her lips, and she moved out into the bitter cold. Yes, Zach excited her more than Dwight did. But that didn't mean they could really see each other. She'd said nothing to anyone about who Zach really was, but she knew her brothers would find out eventually.

And then war would break out.

"Hey," Zach said just as easily. "I was just thinking."

"Of what?"

"You said you used to be a private chef, right?"

"Yes." Confusion ran through her. What did that have to do with anything?

"What if I hired you to come work for me?" he asked. "I have a small farm, but I'm busy a lot of the time. I don't cook for myself much."

Celia paused right in the middle of the parking lot, though the temperature wouldn't allow her to stand still for long. "What?"

"I can pay you just as well as Graham," he said.

It wasn't about the money. Celia didn't need Zach's money. *Bored and rich.* Was he playing a game with her?

"I don't know," she said. She hated the words, because they were all she'd been thinking for days. Could she have a relationship with Zach? She didn't know. Could she somehow move past the family feud? She didn't know. Could she even love someone again?

She simply didn't know.

"Well, I'm at Saltgrass Farms in Dog Valley," he said. "And I'd take you any days you aren't already working at the lodge."

Celia hesitated long enough that someone honked their horn. She lifted her hand in apology and got moving again. "Are you bored right now?"

"What?"

"It's just that you said you were bored and rich. Is this some sort of trick?" Wasn't that what her father had always said about the Zuckermans? They were tricky.

"It's not a trick," he said. "Though the thought did cross my mind that if someone has a problem with our relationship, I can simply say you're working for me."

"And how would that be better than being your...." She couldn't even say the word. "How would that be better?" She unlocked her car and got inside, starting it quickly and adjusting the heater to blow.

"I don't know," he said, a heavy sigh accompanying the words. "All I know is I want to see you again, and maybe if you came to make me lunch or dinner at my farm, we could stay out of the public eye, as you mentioned."

She had said that she'd gone to Dog Valley to stay off

the radar here in Coral Canyon. "I'll have to check my schedule at Whiskey Mountain," she said.

"Of course." Zach sounded like he wouldn't settle for anything less. "What are you doing today?"

"I just got out of church," she said. "And I'm cooking Sunday dinner up at the lodge."

"Mm," he said, and she didn't know him well enough to know if he was distracted or simply didn't have an audible word to say.

"So you'll let me know your schedule and if you want the job," he said.

"I'll let you know."

"Great. Talk to you later." The call ended, and Celia looked at her phone, easily a half-dozen questions running through her mind now.

"That was weird." She put the car in gear and drove about as far away from the canyon as she could get. Once she had her slow cooker and all of her ingredients in the truck of her car, she said, "All right, Grizz. Let's load up."

The black Lab jumped into the front passenger seat, her companion for the long drive up to the lodge. Once there, Celia busied herself with the meal prep, just like she did every Sunday.

The difference this week was the road her thoughts marched down. Every turn and every road sign held Zach's face—and that was no coincidence.

When Graham arrived, Celia's nerves tripled. She had somewhat of a set schedule here at the lodge, and Graham had never been overly inquisitive about what she did the other days of the week.

So she'd just ask him if she could dictate the schedule a bit more. With Eli back in town, perhaps the family could eat down at his house—Amanda's huge estate— sometimes. Celia could cook there as easily as here.

"Hey, Celia." Graham swept into the kitchen, slipping his arm around her waist and squeezing her the way he did his mother. "Something smells good." He grinned down at her and adjusted his toddler on his hip.

"Pulled pork nachos," she said.

"Receipts?" he asked.

"I have them." She hurried over to her purse and extracted that week's receipts. After handing them to him, she said, "I have another job that's come up. Could we set a more permanent schedule here at the lodge?"

"Sure." Graham didn't even look up from the checkbook where he was writing out her pay and her grocery reimbursement. With a flourish, he ripped off the check and extended it toward her. "What days are you thinking?"

"Sunday here," she said. "Of course. And Monday for family night. Maybe I could do Wednesday and Friday too? That would leave Tuesday, Thursday, and Saturday for—for this new client."

She'd almost said Zach—and then the secret would be blown wide open.

Graham cocked his head slightly, as if he'd noticed the slip. "That sounds fine," he said as Ronnie started to babble. "Come on, bud. Let's go find Mom and tell her you need your diaper changed." He grinned at Celia as he left the kitchen, and she sagged against the countertop in relief.

And this was just her boss. How could she ever tell Mack and Lennox about Zach Zuckerman?

CHAPTER 6

Zach whistled along with the wind as it screamed around the corner of the stable. His horses didn't seem to mind the storm, but Zach had stayed longer than necessary. He didn't want to trek through Mother Nature's fury to get back to the house, and he kept thinking that maybe it would die down a little.

He only owned four horses—a far cry from the race-horse breeding farm Finn ran. Zach had already been over to Finn's place, and his best friend would be home tomorrow. So one more morning of double chores, and Zach could go back to a more settled routine.

More boring, he thought as he fiddled with the reins hanging on the wall. "All right, guys," he said to the horses. June, Harold, Runner, and Queen Anne barely looked at him. "I'll see you in the morning."

He pressed his body weight against the door to get it

to open, and then the wind grabbed it and dang near ripped it off the hinges. Groaning, Zach struggled against the wind to bring the door back closed again. With it finally in place and latched, he kept his head down and hurried through the storm.

His boots had just touched the steps on the back deck that led inside when the hail started. "Really?" he muttered, running now. His adrenaline propelled him all the way inside, and he took of his cowboy hat and shook the pellets from the brim.

"This is insane," he said to the darkening sky outside. It was barely three o'clock, but it looked like he should be getting ready for bed.

He felt exhausted all the way down in his bones, and he didn't even know why. It was Sunday, and he typically had a lighter load of chores on the Sabbath. He sat in church for a couple of hours. Puttered around with the six goats and four horses and his horde of chickens.

True, he'd been working both farms, but Finn had everything down to a science, and his farm practically ran itself.

A cold nose touched his hand, startling him. Zach pulled his fingers away from Ginger, his golden retriever. Well, one of them. "You guys hungry?"

He turned from the windows to find all five dogs looking at him. Two of his, and all three of Finn's. He chuckled at the sight of them and moved into the kitchen to put together their meal. They had dry dog food, but they'd barely touched it, almost as if they knew he'd break out the carton of eggs and start scrambling.

As he did exactly that, he sang a hymn from church that day, a measure of happiness moving through him. He knew he was a simple man, with a simple life, and he actually liked that.

He'd lived the bigwig life, with shiny shoes and silk ties. It wasn't a bad life either, but it brought more pressure than he wanted on a Sunday afternoon.

Several minutes later, he split the ham and cheese omelet between five plates and set them down for the dogs. "Wait," he told them in his most commanding voice. Ginger whined, but she held her position. Maple just looked at him with her big, beautiful brown eyes.

Finn's dogs all stared at the plates, used to this drill by now.

"All right," Zach said, stepping out of the way lest he get run over by the stampede of five dogs, each weighing more than sixty pounds. They each took a plate without much argument, and the sliding of plates against the floor and slurping of food commenced.

Zach chuckled at them, glad he could make them so happy with something so easy. He cleaned up the pan, the glass in the window above the sink rattling in the wind. The hail had stopped, but Zach knew the snow was coming. Probably a lot of it.

Celia hadn't seemed too keen on becoming his personal chef, and the weather would probably keep her down in Coral Canyon all week. His heart constricted painfully at the thought of not being able to see her.

But he had a big truck with four-wheel-drive, and maybe he'd go see Owen this week. Check out things on the farm where he'd grown up and then stop by Celia's on the way home. Of course, he had no idea where she lived. Or if she'd even want him at her house.

He filled a glass with ice and water and walked into the library. Really just an office with a lot of books along two of the walls, this room often found Zach when he needed to do finances for the farm—or when he wanted to relax with a jigsaw puzzle.

He'd bought a huge puzzle last time he'd been in Washington, D.C. to visit Abby. It would eventually be the shape of the United States, and depicted all of the National Monuments and Parks around the country.

He'd need a whole room just to display it, and he'd finished Yosemite, Glacier, and several other sections. For the past few weeks, he'd been working on the Grand Canyon, and he looked down at all the reddish-orange pieces.

From somewhere else in the house, his phone chimed. He ignored it and started touching pieces, almost as if they could speak to him and let him know they were the ones he needed.

"Jennie, play Classical Favorites," he said, and a moment later the Internet radio speaker began playing a violin concerto. With the heater blowing, and the storm contained outside, peace filled Zach from top to bottom.

The dogs finished eating, and all five of them came into the library for their afternoon snoozes. Amidst snoring and cellos, Zach fitted together piece after piece, his mind moving slowly through his options with Celia.

If she really didn't want anyone in Coral Canyon to know about their relationship, taking the private chef job would be ideal. But perhaps she didn't want to work for him. It would add a new level to their relationship, and Zach finally leaned away from the table.

"If she wants to have a relationship at all."

But she had seemed interested, and they'd left the diner on good terms. She'd said she'd had fun. He'd asked her out again. No, they didn't have anything on the schedule. Maybe she'd changed her mind.

He looked down at the puzzle, bored with it now. Sighing, he got up and walked over to the window that looked across the front yard. Surprise tripped through him as he found a figure hurrying up his front sidewalk.

Who in the world would be out in this storm?

He moved toward the exit so he could open the front door for whoever it was, as they shouldn't be outside for long in this weather. The doorbell rang as he turned the corner, and he hurried to yank open the door.

"Zach," Celia said, plenty of air in her voice.

"Celia?" He grabbed her by the elbow and towed her inside while the wind tried to pull the door outside. "Come in. What are you doing here?" He closed the door, a shiver moving through his whole system.

Celia was here.

Here.

At his house.

"How did you find my farm?"

"You told me the name of it," she said, shaking her jacket to get rid of the snowflakes that had landed there. She held up a big pot. "I brought dinner."

A smile cracked Zach's face, and his heartbeat started blitzing around inside his chest. "You brought dinner."

She smiled too. "Yeah," she said slowly. "I was thinking maybe I'd take that job."

Laughter started in Zach's throat, and he let it out. "All right, then," he said. "Come on back to the kitchen." He started that way, but Celia paused at the door to the library.

"You have five dogs?"

"Just two," he said. "Three are Finn's, and he and Amanda won't be home until tomorrow." He reached down and stroked Maple's head. "The two golden retrievers are mine."

Celia's eyes met his, and pure joy resided there. "I left my dog in the truck. Could I bring him in?"

"Of course," Zach said. "He'll freeze out there anyway." He cocked his head at her. "Why didn't you just bring him with you in the first place?"

"I wasn't even sure you were home," she said. "I've texted you a few times, and you didn't answer."

His phone had gone off a couple of times, and instant regret hit him. "I'll get him." He started for the kitchen, where he'd hung his coat when he'd come in from the farm. "What's his name?"

"Grizz," she said, following him. "He's a black Lab puppy."

Zach nodded at her. "Use anything you want. I'll be back in a second." He went out through the garage, opening it to find her sedan parked in his driveway. The snow fell fast and furious, and he stood on the cusp of the garage and looked up into the sky.

If Celia stayed for any length of time, she wouldn't be leaving tonight. The idea of her staying with him through the storm struck fear and excitement within him. The feelings didn't quite mesh, and he wasn't sure what to do with them.

He did know he could take on another dog without a problem, so he stepped over to the passenger side to find the little black pup eager to meet him. He laughed as Grizz licked his hands and then his face when he picked him up.

No sense in getting the dog soaking wet just to come into the house. "There you go, boy," he said, setting the dog down once they'd gone inside. Zach hit the button to close the garage, and he peeled his wet coat from his shoulders.

"It's snowing hard," he said, approaching Celia in the kitchen slowly.

"Yeah," she said. "Started just as I pulled into town." She barely glanced up from the rolls in front of her. She worked with a serrated knife easily, and Zach really liked her presence in his home. "As soon as I finish these, I want a tour." She met his eye for a moment, a smile on her face.

"Celia," he said, and she paused in the slicing.

"Yeah?"

"If you stay even five more minutes, you won't be leaving Dog Valley tonight." He cleared his throat, and he didn't even care what that said about him. He liked this woman, and he'd be more than happy if she stayed. But she should know what she was choosing.

"You think so?"

"Definitely." He watched her move to the back doors that led onto the deck and look outside.

She turned back to him, determination in those beautiful eyes. "Well, I want to stay, so I guess I better have that tour now so I know where I'm sleeping tonight."

Zach ducked his head, glad he wore a cowboy hat all the time. He wasn't sure he concealed his smile all that much, but it didn't matter. She'd said the magic words.

I want to stay.

"All right," he said, his voice a bit on the gruff side. "So this is the kitchen and dining room. There's a little utility room around the corner there, but I don't use it much. I just came in from the garage—which you can pull your car in, if you'd like." He extended his hand toward her. "In fact, give me your keys, and I'll do it right now."

She stepped over to her discarded coat and pulled her keys from the pocket.

"Be right back." He left her in the kitchen for the

second time and went back into the garage. He could barely fold himself behind the wheel of her car, but he managed to get it into the garage.

Back in the house again, he found all six dogs sitting in a circle around Celia while she fed each one little bits of meat, one at a time.

Zach paused, the scene before him almost surreal. Celia was a steady force he hadn't known he needed in his life. He felt like things in his life were going well, but he simply hadn't realized that he still had a hole in his life where a woman should be.

A good, strong, faithful, beautiful woman like Celia Armstrong.

The vein in his neck throbbed as he thought about Brandon, but no guilt came. No regret. His friend would want his wife taken care of, and for the first time in a while, Zach wanted to take care of more than dogs, horses, and goats.

He wanted to take care of Celia, and that rendered him still and silent, because he had no idea how to do that.

CHAPTER 7

"Oh, you've done it now," Zach said, and Celia looked up from the circle of dogs. He wore such happiness on his face, making him twice as handsome as he already was. "You shouldn't have fed them. They won't leave you alone now."

She nodded toward the five plates on the floor. "I suppose you would know." She cocked her eyebrows at him, hoping it came off as flirtatious and not challenging. "And you said you didn't cook."

"Well, I know how to scramble an egg," he said. "Doesn't mean I want to do it."

"I talked to Graham at the lodge," she said. "I can come on Tuesdays, Thursdays, and Saturdays, if you really want me to cook for you." She still wasn't sure what Zach's motives were.

"I do," he said quickly. "What do you do? Dinner? Lunch?"

"Whatever you want," she said. "I get reimbursed for all my groceries, and I'm not cheap, Mister." She pressed one palm against his chest, freezing in that moment.

He looked down at her hand and then back into her eyes, something sizzling striking the space between them. "I can pay you," he said. "Name the price."

Celia's mind had gone blank.

"Do you cook for dogs too?"

The question snapped her back to reality, and she giggled. Actually giggled, as if she were a much younger woman. She knew she wasn't, though, and that caused her to step back from Zach, taking her hand with her.

"I can cook for the dogs," she said. "Are they picky?"

"Absolutely not," Zach said, taking a micro-step closer to her, as if he felt the chill Celia did now that she wasn't touching him. "I'm not either, by the way."

"You'll get to keep all the leftovers," she said. "It's your food. So I can come make lunch on Tuesdays. That should get you through to Thursday night. I could do dinner then. And then come for lunch or dinner on Saturday."

A beat of silence filled the expansive kitchen before he said, "What about both on Saturdays?"

Celia's gaze flew to his again, and plenty of desire waved at her from within the depths of his dark eyes. She couldn't help seizing onto it. Memorizing this way he looked at her. No one had looked at her like this for so, so long.

Of course, she hadn't dated. She'd chosen the life she'd

had, and she knew it. She also knew what she'd just chosen tonight. And for the foreseeable future.

"Let's leave Saturday open," she said. "Any of it is changeable. If you find you don't want me to come as often, that's okay too."

Zach reached out and touched her fingers, sending a pulse of heat up her arm. "I want you to come as often as possible."

Celia's head swam with the nearness of him. The strong scent of his cologne. The roughness of his hand as he fully took hers in his. "Is this crazy?" she asked, her voice breathless. She felt a little crazy, just as she had for the long drive here.

She usually stayed up at the lodge for the full afternoon, enjoying the children as they played. She liked having adult conversations and being involved in everyone's life. They treated her like their own mothers, and she loved everyone who came to the lodge.

But today, she'd felt the need to leave and come see Zach. Spend more time with him. Satisfy the craving and see if it went away, or if it would grow.

And right now, she definitely felt it growing. Expanding and seething within her until she laid her cheek against his chest.

He brought his other arm around her, resting his hand lightly on her waist. A blip of self-consciousness moved through her, as she knew she wasn't the thinnest woman around. After all, she had to taste everything she made. But Zach didn't recoil from her.

"If it's crazy," he whispered. "I don't care."

In that moment, Celia didn't either. Her family wasn't here. His wasn't either. And for a few minutes, it felt like maybe they could be together on this farm, in this town.

He cleared his throat and stepped back, and a rush of awkwardness moved through Celia. "So there are three bedrooms on this level," he said. "Let me show you."

He took her back down the hall toward the front door. "Library over there. I was doing a puzzle when you arrived. There's a bathroom right next door." He turned to the other side of the hall. "Two bedrooms here, with another bathroom between them." He faced her. "You can sleep in either of these. My kids stay here when they come."

"How often do they come?"

"Not that often," he said with a smile. "But I think the rooms are decently clean, and I always put on clean sheets after someone stays, so they're ready whenever anyone needs them."

"So organized," she teased, and she slipped her hand back into his as he turned to go down a hall.

"Living room, obviously," he said. "Only this main level is finished. The basement is empty."

"It's pretty big," she said.

"Three thousand square feet," he said. "And it's just me. Well, and the dogs." He paused in the doorway. "This is my room. Bathroom to the left. Big closet back there that could probably be another bedroom."

"Probably." She chuckled, but she didn't go inside. His bed was made, and that spoke volumes about a man.

"I have a huge deck that's really nice in the summer," he said, taking her back into the living room, where he had two comfortable-looking couches. "The yard's decent. Farm back there." He nodded out the windows, but the storm obscured anything she might have been able to see.

"This is nice," she said. "Different than where you grew up."

"Oh, yeah," he said. "No one wants to have to fight for the single bathroom." He grinned at her. "Sometimes I can't believe we really only had one bathroom in our whole house. Even my parents used it." He shook his head like such a thing was unfathomable, and Celia just smiled at him.

"My place is much smaller than this," she said, suddenly nervous for him to ever come to her house.

"I can't wait to see it," he said. "Maybe after we've told everyone about us."

"Maybe," she said. "I don't quite know how to start that conversation with my brothers." She moved into the kitchen, Zach going with her. She resumed the slicing of the rolls and reached for the tongs to stir the meat. "This is ready." She glanced up at him. "Are you hungry?"

"Always," he said, beaming at her.

Warmth filled Celia. She could feed people. She knew she was good at it, and she derived great joy from doing it. So she got to work getting down plates and pulling out silverware in Zach's kitchen while he sat at the bar and watched her.

When she finally sat down next to him, he took her hand in his again and lifted it to his lips. "I'm so glad you came," he said.

"Me too," she said. "Thanks for letting me stay here tonight, too."

"Mm." He gazed at her, and strange and new emotions spiraled through Celia. "I'll pray," he said next, and she took the excuse to close her eyes. She needed to figure out what all of these things inside her heart and mind meant, and fast.

Reagan would know, and Celia determined to call her daughter the moment she was alone.

৩%৩

LATER THAT NIGHT—CELIA finally sat up as the movie ended. "I should get to bed."

Zach yawned too, but he stayed right where he sat on the couch. "You've got everything?"

"Nothing to get, right?" She gave him a soft smile, as it was much later than she normally stayed up. At least she had Grizz with her, so she didn't have to worry about who would take care of him while she was snowed in.

"I put a new toothbrush in the bathroom," he said. "Toothpaste too. Towels in there. Everything is set in the bedroom." He smiled at her too, and Celia's mind went into overdrive. Fantasies of kissing him drove through her imagination, and she was eternally glad he couldn't read minds.

"Thanks. See you in the morning."

"No rush to get up," he said. "I think the storm has pretty much decided to stay here and drop everything it has."

"Probably." She pushed herself up and started across the room, her legs protesting at the movement. She felt and surely looked like an old lady, but she didn't turn back. Embarrassment heated her face, but she didn't care. Behind her, Zach groaned as he got up, and the sound made her smile.

He wasn't terribly young either.

She brushed her teeth and ran the water hot to wash her face. Once alone behind the locked door of the bedroom, she pulled out her phone. Thankfully, she kept a charging cable in her car, and Zach had loaned her a plug.

It was just after ten o'clock, but somehow it felt so much later than that. The last several hours with Zach felt like a dream, so far removed from her reality, she wasn't sure she'd lived them.

Can I call you real quick? She sent the message zipping across the miles to her daughter Reagan.

Sure. I'm up.

Of course she was. Reagan had always been a night-owl, something Celia had never truly appreciated until that moment.

Her nerves zipped along her skin as the phone rang, and then her daughter said, "Heya, Momma. What's up?"

Music played in the background, but it wasn't the club kind. Less harsh, and definitely less bass.

"Oh, I don't know," Celia said, suddenly feeling foolish.

"You don't know?" Reagan gave a short laugh. "Right. Did you go out with that guy and now you're worried about it?"

"No," Celia said, though her daughter had gotten part of it right. "I mean, not really worried. I wouldn't say worried."

Reagan laughed again, longer and with more happiness this time. "Mom, start at the beginning."

Celia did, but she went fast, only taking a few moments to talk about lunch at the diner. She moved on to Zach asking her to be his personal chef, and her insane desire to see him that very day.

"And now I'm snowed in at his place, and I don't know, Rae." She exhaled heavily. "I don't know how I feel."

"Who says you have to know?" Reagan asked. "Mom, it's called *dating.*"

"I just haven't done anything like this in so long." Celia's desperation came through in every syllable. "I mean, is it normal to want to spend a lot of time with him? What if I'm smothering him?"

"Mom, this is totally normal. You like him, and you want to get to know him. You're not smothering him. He feels the same way you do."

"He does?"

"Yes," Reagan said with a chuckle. "Mom, he didn't

want to hire you as his personal chef. He wanted to see you more often."

Celia had known that. "So should I not take the job?"

"Do you need the job?"

"No."

"Then, no, Mom. Don't take the job. Simply tell him you'll come cook for him whenever he wants, and then do that."

Celia looked around at the generic furnishings in the room. It almost felt like a hotel, with a watercolor of flowers on the wall and soft linens on the bed. She wasn't sure what she was searching for, but she knew it wasn't in this room.

"Okay," she finally said. "Thanks, Rae. Love you."

"Just be you, Mom," Reagan said. "It'll all be fine." They said good-bye and hung up, but Celia didn't put her phone away.

She fired off a text to Zach. *I don't want to be your personal chef.*

Swallowing, she hurried to type out the rest of the message. *I'll just come make you lunch or dinner whenever you want. Sound good?*

Her phone indicated that he was typing. Then that message went away. Her phone buzzed in her hand.

Zach was calling her.

CHAPTER 8

"You don't want the job?" he asked, knowing Celia had taken the bedroom right on the other side of the wall where he stood. He'd designed the house with his architect, and if he stood in the corner of the room beside his bathroom, eight inches away sat the nightstand he'd put in the guest bedroom where Celia was staying.

Eight inches.

So close, and yet so far away.

"No," she said with a sigh. "You don't need to pay me to come spend time with you."

"I'm not," he said instantly. "I'm paying you to come cook for me. You don't want me to buy the groceries?"

"Zach," Celia said, her voice serious and even. He wished he could see her face. Touch her cheek. Hold her close, like he'd done while they watched a movie together on his couch. Two of them, in fact.

She'd made popcorn, and he'd brought in a huge container of chocolate ice cream from the freezer in the garage. It had been one of the very best Sunday evenings of his life.

"Celia," he said.

"I don't think you really want a private chef."

He didn't, but he didn't want to admit it. So he remained silent. She seemed like she had something to say anyway.

"I just want to spend time with you." Her voice dropped to a whisper. "Not in Coral Canyon."

"That's what I was trying to do," he said. "Give you a reason to come up here without it seeming like you were running off to see your secret boyfriend." He pulled in a breath. Had he just said the word *boyfriend*? Out loud?

He felt way too old to bear the label of boyfriend. And yet, he really wanted to be Celia's boyfriend.

She'd asked earlier if their relationship was crazy, and Zach hadn't thought so then. But now, he felt a little insane for his thoughts. He'd met this woman a week ago. Sure, he'd known her growing up. Sort of. She was an Abbott, and he hated them all on principle.

"It's a good reason," she admitted. "Logical."

"If you don't want me to pay you, fine," he said. "I'll still pay for the groceries, and I'd love to see you...." He cleared his throat. He wanted to see her every day. But it was a long drive from Dog Valley to Whiskey Mountain Lodge. He knew. He'd done it for the wedding.

"Whenever you can come," he finished lamely. "And I

can come to Coral Canyon, Celia. We won't be able to hide forever."

"I know," she said. "But I want to talk to my brothers first."

"That's fine," he said, repeating something they'd already talked about over pulled pork sandwiches. He was going to feel out Owen. Learn more about the feud. She was going to do the same on her side of the line. See what Mack and Lennox had to say. Find out if the animosity between the two families had diminished at all now that her father had passed.

Their plans had all sounded great with barbecue sauce and coleslaw.

"Okay," she said. "That was all. I just...I told you hadn't dated since Brandon. I don't know what I'm doing."

He chuckled, his affection for this good woman soaring. "You're doing fine, sweetheart," he said. "I'll see you in the morning."

"Night," she said, and Zach hung up, fierce imaginations of kissing her right after she said that next time.

Next time, he promised himself.

He plugged in his phone, another yawn coursing through his whole body. Owen wouldn't be awake. He'd told Celia she could call early but not late, and such was the life of a farmer. He texted his brother anyway.

Would love to come see you this week and catch up. When's a good day?

ZACH GRIPPED the steering wheel as he went up the canyon to Whiskey Mountain Lodge. The snow had relented during the night, but Celia's small sedan couldn't handle the eight inches Wyoming had taken.

His truck could, however, and he'd driven her to the lodge for the day. The ride had been full of conversation and smiles, and Zach hadn't even realized that almost an hour had passed.

As the lodge came into view, Celia said, "I can be done any time after three," she said. "Do you want to just text me?"

"Sure," he said, feeling the truck slide a bit as he drove into the parking lot. The lodge had steam drifting up from a pipe in the roof, but otherwise, it looked calm and quiet. "I'm talking to Owen today."

He pulled under the overhang that protected the front door of the lodge and put the truck in park.

"Are you—what are you going to tell him?"

Zach sighed. "I haven't worked it all out yet." He glanced at her, a playful smile on his face. "I think I might just generally see what he thinks about Abbotts in general."

Celia nodded, tight lines appearing around her eyes. Zach knew the worries of parenthood, and he could see the years she'd spent laboring with her daughters right there on her face. He wondered what each line held exactly, and he hoped he could find out.

In that moment, he didn't much care what his brother thought of his new girlfriend. "And besides," Zach said. "You're not even an Abbott anymore."

Their eyes met again, and she said, "I have been an Armstrong for a while now."

But Zach knew the technicality wouldn't matter. Owen would still see Celia as the daughter of the Abbotts, a family all Zuckermans were raised to loathe.

"Shouldn't we forgive?" he asked, only realizing when he heard his voice that he'd spoken out loud.

Celia reached over and touched his hand, and Zach easily slid his fingers through hers. The motion felt natural and beautiful, and he squeezed, trying to take every comfort he needed.

"I mean, this feud is stupid. We're Christians. Shouldn't we have forgiven whatever it was long ago?" He looked at her, truly wanting to know what she thought.

"Perhaps," she said gently. "But we don't even really know what the feud is about."

"It was about some land that borders both properties," Zach said, searching his memories. "And water rights."

"Then you know more than me." She removed her hand from his and took a deep breath. "Okay, I better go in before Beau comes to see why I'm just sitting here." She gave him a pretty smile, picked up her purse, and opened the door. A blast of cold air entered, and she muttered against it.

Zach's happiness swelled as he watched her walk to the door and look back at him. He raised his hand to say a silent good-bye, and she smiled again before entering the lodge. He stayed in the truck for another minute, basking in the atmosphere here at this canyon lodge.

"Thank you, Lord," he said, his voice barely reaching his own ears. He knew God would hear him though, no matter how loud or how quiet he spoke. He wasn't even sure what he was thankful for—or who he was thankful for—only that he wanted to acknowledge the feeling of gratitude as he felt it.

"Please help me with Owen." He put the truck in gear and added, "And help me get down this canyon without sliding off the road."

Satisfied with his pleas to the Lord, he kept a tight grip on the steering wheel as he inched down the snow-packed roads toward flatter ground. The plows had been out down here, and he relaxed as he started driving down the country roads that would take him to the place where he'd been raised.

A lot of people had farms in Coral Canyon, and homes generally sat several hundred yards apart. He'd always liked exploring his property, hopping fences, and checking out a new place too. As he'd grown older and learned he shouldn't do that, he admired farms from appropriate distances.

He made a left turn and drove slowly down the road that had served as a dividing line between his family and the Abbotts for years. To his right, the Abbott farm spread north and east. To his left, the Zuckerman farm spread south and east. To an outsider, they looked quaint. Beautiful. Similar.

But on the inside, Zach knew something seethed and writhed, staining everything and everyone it touched.

He just needed to figure out what that root source of contention was and get rid of it. Easy.

He scoffed at himself and caught sight of a truck moving down the Abbott's lane toward the road he was on. As he neared, he kept his eyes on the driver.

It was Mack Abbott, the oldest of Celia's brothers. Because Zach hadn't spent much of the last thirty years thinking about the Abbotts, he had a hard time remembering how old the man was.

Older than Owen, who was fifty-three. Older than Celia, who was fifty-four. Almost at once, he remembered Celia saying she and Mack were barely a year apart, and he lifted his hand in a hello as he put on his left blinker.

Mack returned the gesture, so either the feud didn't matter, or he didn't recognize Zach.

Zach turned onto his family's lane and immediately looked in his rear-view mirror. Mack's scowl spoke volumes, and Zach almost braked to go back. Maybe two people just needed to sit down and talk.

"And it's not going to be you," he told himself as he continued forward, the snow here deeper than in Dog Valley.

He pulled up to the homestead, where someone had cleared off the driveway, and got out of the truck. The air smelled crisp and clean, and that was one good thing about the snow. Of course, a breath too deep could really burn the lungs, so he didn't waste any time outside.

The front door wasn't locked, and Zach called, "Hello?" as he entered. His mouth watered with the scent of coffee, and his muscles relaxed at the introduction of heat to the surroundings.

"Zach." His brother Owen appeared from down the hall, a friendly smile already on his face. They embraced amidst laughter, and Zach glanced around the house where he'd once lived.

"Everything seems so small," he said.

"I know," Owen said darkly. "I'm getting some remodeling done once spring comes."

"Oh yeah?"

"Yep. Aleah wants to open things up."

"Can't say I disagree with her." Zach had never liked Owen's wife all that much, but he knew how to play nice and get along. "Where is Lee?"

"Shopping," Owen said, getting down a couple of coffee mugs. "Audrey's birthday party is this weekend."

"Oh, right," Zach said. "Fifteen."

Owen flashed a smile, though it certainly wasn't the first birthday party he'd hosted at the farm. He had five children, and Audrey was the youngest.

He put a sugar bowl on the counter and poured Zach a cup of coffee. "So what brings you by? I know it's not to help with the chores in this weather."

Zach chuckled and shook his head. "Nope. I'm already pulling double-duty for my friend while he's out of town."

Owen lifted his mug to his lips, his dark eyes full of questions. Zach had no idea what to say. He took his time stirring entirely too much sugar into his coffee.

"I have a dilemma," he finally said. "I was hoping you could help me with it."

"If I can," Owen said, and Zach saw the overprotective brother he'd always had. Owen did love his family fiercely and would do anything for them.

"I started seeing someone." Zach cleared his throat. "A woman."

A smile bloomed on Owen's face. "Wow. That's a big step for you."

"Yeah." Zach felt flushed all over, and he wanted a cool drink of water instead of this hot coffee. "Anyway, there's a problem with her family." He watched Owen for any type of reaction.

Confusion knitted his brother's brows. "Really? Her family?" He straightened. "Is she twenty years younger than you or something?"

"No," Zach said slowly, wishing he'd brought up the feud first. He didn't see a way he could bring it up now without disclosing who the woman was. "She's actually older than me."

"How much older?"

"Only a few years." Zach squirmed on the barstool and pushed his coffee away. He was fifty years old, for crying out loud. "The problem is, she's an Abbott. Or she used to be."

Owen sucked in a breath that sounded very much like a hiss. "Celia?"

Zach nodded, desperation coursing through him now. "And I'm wondering if you can tell me more about this feud between our families."

Owen paced to the kitchen sink, looked out the window there for what felt like a long time, and then faced Zach again. "They're crooks, Zach. You know that, right?"

"I didn't know that," he said evenly.

"They claimed to own the exact piece of land where the water flowed to our farm from the north," Owen said, his face an angry mask of fire. His eyes blazed with the hatred Zach could feel streaming from him.

"When did this happen?" Zach asked.

"Right when Gramps was taking over the farm," Owen said. "And suddenly, the Abbotts owned another ten acres of land and we had no way to water our crops."

Zach didn't want to point fingers or escalate anything. "But we obviously still water our crops."

"Yeah," Owen clipped out. "We had to buy a whole new set of rights, and I just barely finished paying for them."

Decades of debt. Zach nodded, his heart heavy. A single ray of hope shone through him though. "So it could be over. I mean, it's been what? A hundred years?" Their grandfather had taken over the farm when their dad was three or four years old.

"It'll never be over," Owen said. "They caused us grief

for a long time." He shook his head. "You should find yourself a new girlfriend."

"She's not my girlfriend," Zach said quickly just to avoid further argument. "I just started seeing her."

"Yeah, well, end it." Owen slammed his coffee mug on the kitchen counter. "I have work to do." He stormed out of the kitchen, exactly as he'd done for many years when things didn't go his way.

Zach stayed even after the back door had slammed closed and he'd watched his brother move down the paths in the snow to the outbuildings on the farm.

"Help him forgive," he whispered to the faint reflection of himself in the glass. But he knew that would take a miracle, and while Zach believed in those, he hadn't seen one in his own life for a long time.

CHAPTER 9

Celia scrolled to the next page on the film she'd requested from the library. The air held the general sense of dust, as if no one ever used these machines to look at these old documents anymore. And they probably didn't.

But the history of Coral Canyon hadn't been completely digitized yet, and it wasn't available on the computer. So she sat at the microfiche station and scrolled, the white letters on black backgrounds starting to wear on her eyes.

Zach had told her about the root of the feud between their two families, and Celia had started researching. Maybe she just didn't want her family to be the villains. Maybe she needed to justify what they'd done.

No matter what, she had an affinity for history, and she'd loved learning about the people that had come before her, the places they'd lived, and the laws they'd had to uphold. She'd first gone to her History of Coral Canyon hardcover book, and she'd learned that ninety-seven years ago, new laws for farmers had been introduced.

That had to be close to the time her family had allegedly gained ten more acres on their farm, effectively cutting the Zuckermans off from their water rights.

She hadn't spoken to Lennox or Mack, so she wasn't sure what the story was on her side yet. She wanted to be armed with as much knowledge as possible before she approached them.

Zach had not been happy when he'd picked her up earlier that week. He hadn't broken things off with her, but he'd been strangely distant, and she'd skipped driving to Dog Valley to spend Saturday with him in favor of holing up here in the library.

He wanted a solution to the problem as much as she did, and he'd put out calls to his friends still in real estate to find someone who sold water rights and what was happening in Coral Canyon at the time.

She'd learned that Wyoming had since moved to a permit system, and that both her family and Zach's had permits with the state to use the water they'd been fighting over. So she wasn't sure what water rights Owen had just paid off, and neither was Zach.

The whole thing made her head hurt. And yet, she continued to scroll, searching for something in the headlines that would give her another piece of the puzzle. She wasn't even sure what to look for, what words, what announcements.

She took out the roll of film when it finished and inserted the next one. As it came to life, right there at the top sat the headline *Two Local Farmers Vie For Water*.

Her great-grandfather's picture stared back at her, and Celia couldn't read fast enough. "When the state implemented it's new law, all riparian land and water had to be claimed or else it was lost."

She went on to read that if her great-grandfather hadn't claimed that extra ten acres, neither farm would've had water.

"We want to use the water we have for decades," she read. "Augustus Zuckerman said. If he takes all the land there, we have nothing. Zuckerman goes on to say that he offered to split the cost of the land with Abbott, who refused."

She leaned away from the article, her heartbeat thrashing through her veins. "It was your family's fault," she said. "Why couldn't they have just shared with the Zuckermans?" It seemed like that was what the two farms and families had done previous to the new law.

Looking up toward the ceiling, she imagined herself in the room with her great-grandfather. "Why?"

"Are you finding everything okay?" the librarian asked, interrupting Celia's heart-to-heart with her dead ancestor.

"Yes," she said. "If I wanted to print this, how could I do that?" She indicated the story still on the screen of the microfiche.

"Oh, that's easy," Amelia said. "You just push that

button right there." She pointed to a big, black button on the side of the machine.

"Great, thanks." Celia printed out the article, paid for it, and hurried out of the library. Armed with more answers—and many more questions—she felt one step closer to a resolution.

She could only hope and pray that the resolution included keeping Zach in her life. She sure did like him, and she didn't want something from almost a century ago to keep them apart.

No, she didn't know if *everything* would work out between them, but until she knew that it wouldn't, she wanted to keep all her options open.

৩৵৩

"So you're saying my family has a right to feel jilted." Zach straightened, the piping bag of green frosting still clutched in his hand.

Celia had just finished explaining everything she'd found at the library and in her Coral Canyon history book. "It seems so," she said miserably. She couldn't even get into the spirit of St. Patrick's Day, though she'd signed them up for this cookie-decorating class only a few days ago.

"Wow," he said. "I was expecting the Zuckermans to be wrong."

"Were you?" She watched him go back to swirling the frosting over the four-leaf clover-shaped cookie. He hadn't been thrilled about this cooking class, but Celia wanted to get out of his house. Out of hers. Out of the lodge.

Maybe the senior citizens center in Dog Valley wasn't Zach's first choice, but he seemed to be enjoying himself. And hey, he had the silver specks in his hair to prove he belonged there.

"Yes," he said simply. "My father was a hothead. My brothers are too, especially Owen."

"Has he asked about me since you talked to him?"

"Not for a few days," Zach said.

"What did you tell him?"

Zach wouldn't look up from the cookie, and Celia's heart pushed out two extra beats, then three.

"Zach?"

He'd never answered her questions about how his meeting with his brother had gone. Not directly. He dodged. He changed the subject. He gave one-liners and moved on to something else.

His visit to his brother and his childhood farm had happened over a week ago. She'd shown up that morning as scheduled and put lunch in the slow cooker before surprising Zach with this mid-afternoon cookie-decorating class.

He set down the green frosting and picked up a white bag with a skinny tip. "I maybe made a mistake."

Celia couldn't focus on her own decorating anymore. "A mistake? What did you say?"

Zach wore a guilty look in those dreamy eyes, and Celia couldn't believe he hadn't told her all of this last week. "I should've just asked about the feud, but I wasn't sure how. I told him I was seeing someone, and well, through everything else that was said, he knows it's you."

She fell back a step, trying to absorb what he'd said. She couldn't breathe and think and speak at the same time, so she just stood there and stared at him.

"It's fine," Zach said, peering down at his cookie again as a red flush stained his neck and ears.

"Fine?" Celia repeated. "How is it fine?" She hadn't said a word to Lennox or Mack, and if Owen did....

They don't talk to one another, she reminded herself. Owen wouldn't go spreading gossip to the cowboys across the street that he hated.

"I told him you weren't my girlfriend."

If anything, the words stabbed her deeper, driving all the way through her heart. She blinked, trying to make sense of them. "Wha—what?"

No, she and Zach hadn't put labels on their relationship, but she was fifty-four-years-old. She wasn't dating anyone else, and if anyone had asked her who Zach was, she'd have said he was her boyfriend.

In fact, she'd told Ruth and Reagan just on Sunday evening that he was her boyfriend.

Zach looked up, finally realizing that Celia had turned into a statue. She searched his face, trying to find the answers she wanted. Problem was, she didn't know what she wanted to hear him say.

Oh, yes, she did.

"Am I your girlfriend?" she asked, lifting her chin. He'd

have to flat-out say no for her to believe him. The man texted and called her every day. He held her hand whenever they were together. She'd snuggled into his side more times than she could count.

His throat worked, but no sound came out of his mouth. He finally came up with, "I mean, I'm not seeing anyone else."

Celia shook her head. "That's not good enough." She couldn't believe she was having this conversation with him, with dozens of other people around. A peal of laughter came from the next table over, drawing her attention.

The other guests at this cookie decorating event seemed to be absorbed in their own tasks. Their family members had come, and she hoped her grandchildren and great-grandchildren would come visit her when she got old enough to live in a place like this.

"Celia." Zach put down his frosting bag and stepped toward her. When he said her name like that, soft and sincere, and full of emotion, she had no defense against him. "If anyone else was asking, I would have said you were my girlfriend." A small smile touched his lips, and he ducked his head.

That cowboy hat came between them, and while Celia really loved the look, she really wanted to see his eyes in this moment.

She reached up and took off his hat. That got him to look at her, all kinds of emotions swirling in the dark depths of his eyes. "Really?"

"Really."

Celia enjoyed the light as it spread through her soul, and she wanted to hold onto it for a long time. She felt warm from head to toe, and she wished she wasn't standing only a few feet away from someone she'd met an hour ago. Her gaze dropped to Zach's mouth, and she thought about kissing him—not for the first time.

"Can I have my hat back?"

Giddiness pranced through Celia, and she stepped back and handed him his hat. He settled it back on his head and looked at her again. "So we're okay?"

Celia nodded, though she still experienced a lingering sting somewhere behind her lungs. "You really told him we weren't dating?"

Zach sighed and squeezed the frosting bag like he wanted to choke the life out of it. "I mean, he was pretty angry. I probably would've told him anything." He looked down at the completed cookies on their table and sighed. "He told me I should end things with you."

Celia didn't know what to say. That conversation between Zach and his brother was over a week old, and he hadn't broken up with her. That meant something, right?

"You two are so cute," an aged voice said. "Don't worry about whoever said you should break-up with her, son. It's clear you belong together."

Celia swung her attention to the older gentleman at their table. She'd forgotten he was even there, but now she gave him a smile. He didn't have family with him that day, and a nurse had pushed him to the table and introduced him as Darrel.

Zach chuckled and went back to the decorating. "You think so, Darrel?"

"Oh, I know a good thing when I see it. My Suzannah was such a sweet thing."

Celia smiled then too, letting the old man take the conversation from serious things. But she kept them all close, tucked away inside her heart.

That night, as she knelt beside the bed, her head bent, she asked the Lord to guide her. "Help me take the first step," she said. "And then another, and then another. Put my feet where they should be. Help my eyes to see."

She didn't know what else she could possibly ask for, and God had never led her somewhere she shouldn't be. No, He hadn't always given her exactly what she wanted. If that were true, Brandon wouldn't have died.

But He had put people in her life right when she needed them. Friends. Family. Neighbors. Pastors.

And maybe, just maybe, He had put Zach in her life when we he needed to be there too. Until God told her otherwise, she was going to keep taking one more step. And then one more.

"And help me know what to say to Lennox and Mack." She rolled her shoulders, feeling the weight of the last ninety-seven years there. "Help us all to forgive."

CHAPTER 10

Zach waited on Finn's doorstep, wishing he could duck inside. But he'd already tried the doorknob, and it was locked. He'd heard the doorbell chime through the house, and still no one had come.

He clutched the cake Celia had made the day before, prepared to tell his friends where he'd gotten it if they asked. And of course, they would ask.

If they ever answered the door.

He shivered as a blast of wind shook the house in front of him, and he wondered if Mother Nature had missed the memo that said it was almost April. He and Celia had spent loads of time together at his house on the farm, and she'd even started coming out into the barns with him. She'd met all the horses and goats, and he'd even ventured down to Coral Canyon a time or two to spend a Saturday night with her.

They didn't go out, but Celia could recreate any restaurant recipe from scratch, and Zach swore he'd gained ten pounds since he'd started seeing her.

She hadn't said anything to her brothers, and Zach hadn't gone to see Owen again. His brother had only texted once since the cookie decorating incident, and Zach had said that he wasn't quite ready to be dating again.

It was partially true, and he and Celia were moving very slow. He didn't mind, as she was busy with her job at the lodge and her daughter's upcoming wedding.

Finally, the door unlatched in front of him, revealing Finn and Amanda. "Come in." Finn backed up, a glow about his face that Zach hadn't seen before.

"I brought a cake," he said, handing it off to Amanda.

She looked at it and then him. "This looks amazing. What kind is it?" She started for the kitchen, and Zach followed her while Finn closed the door.

Zach fumbled for what Celia had called it. "Cookie Monster...and Cream."

She nearly fell down she stopped so fast. "Cookie Monsters and Cream?" She turned back to him, her blue eyes razor sharp.

"Yes, ma'am." Zach was supremely glad he wasn't this woman's son, though in that moment, he felt like he was. She could see every truth and every lie he'd ever told with those eyes.

"Where did you get this?" she asked.

"It's a cake, dear." Finn took it from her with a smile. "Why are you grilling him?"

"I'm not grilling him." She loosened up and continued into the kitchen, leaning closer to Finn to whisper something.

Finn flinched, and Zach braced himself for the next question. He knew it was coming. Finn didn't have too many subtle bones in his body.

"Are you seeing someone?" he finally asked, his eyes wide and filled with surprise.

And there it was.

"As a matter of fact," Zach said. "I am. She made the cake."

"I can't believe she hasn't told me," Amanda said.

"You know who it is?" Finn looked back and forth between Zach and his wife.

"Of course," Amanda said. "It's Celia. She's the only one I've ever seen make a Cookie Monsters and Cream cake." Her fingers flew over her screen before Zach could explain anything. Amanda looked up. "How long?"

"Since the wedding," he said.

"Of course. You were watching her at the wedding." Finn's face burst into a grin, and he nodded like Zach had done something miraculous by getting a woman to go out with him. He probably had, but it wasn't like he and Celia went out that much.

"It's kind of a secret," he said as Amanda frowned at her phone. "Our families don't get along. There's been this feud for almost one hundred years."

"Intriguing," Finn said, and Zach wished he thought so.

"Feud?" Amanda repeated. "What does that mean?"

"It means we haven't really told anyone we're dating." Zach shrugged out of his coat and hung it on a peg near the door that led to the garage. "So don't feel bad she hasn't told you. She hasn't told anyone but her kids."

"Confirmed," Amanda said, lifting her phone. "Since the wedding." She grinned at Finn and then Zach. "I'm so happy for you two."

"It's new," Zach said.

"Why didn't she come with you tonight?" Finn asked.

"She works up at the lodge on Sundays," he said. "And I guess Vi Christopherson was having a big party because she finally brought her twins to church." He looked at Amanda for confirmation on that too.

She nodded. "I took a gift to her yesterday, remember, Finny? We didn't want to go today because it's supposed to snow."

"I can't believe it's going to snow again." Finn looked out the wall of back windows, a dark look in his eyes. "It's time to warm up."

"Amen," Zach said.

"Everything's ready," Amanda said. "Let's say grace, and then I want to hear more about this feud."

Zach looked at her, thinking maybe she could help. How, he didn't know, but he added a silent prayer to the one Finn said over the food that there could be some solution to the feud that allowed him to keep Celia in his life.

"SHE KNEW AS SOON as I said the name of the cake."
Zach smiled at the horses in the barn, though he was on
the phone with Celia. "I didn't know I needed to rename
the cake."

She giggled, and Zach wished she wasn't an hour away,
staying the night in the lodge because of the snow. He
wanted her eight inches away, on the other side of the wall
at his house. Or better, in the same room with him.

The strength of his feelings surprised him, and he kept
them under his tongue.

"Amanda's not a gossip."

"Good," he said. "Because I'm pretty sure she knows
every single person in Coral Canyon."

"Nah," Celia said. "She's been gone a month and there
are tons of new houses going in down here." She laughed
again, the sound muffled like she was trying to keep from
being overheard.

"How was the party?" he asked.

"So good," she said. "The babies are so cute. Vi and
Rose and Lily are all named after flowers, and Vi kept that
tradition. She named them Daisy and Amaryllis. She's
going to call her Mary."

"Very cute," Zach agreed. He measured out the medi-
cine Queen Anne needed, listening as Celia talked more
about the party.

"Amanda and Finn were smart not to stay," she said.
"The wind up here is crazy. We've lost power twice
already."

"Ouch," he said. "Stay warm."

"I will. Hey, I wanted to talk to you about something." She barely had time to breathe before she added, "I want you to come to the lodge next Sunday."

Zach stepped back over to the counter and stilled in his clean-up process. "You do?"

"Yes," she said. "This place is really special to me, and I don't see why I can't include you in it."

"How many people will be there?"

"A lot," she said. "All the Whittaker boys. Their wives and families. The Everetts come every week too. Amanda and Finn."

Zach started tabulating, but lost count after twelve. "So a lot."

"Yes," Celia said, a teasing quality in her voice. "I just said that."

"They don't all live at the lodge."

"No."

"So the potential for word to get around about us is big."

"I'm going to talk to my brothers this week," she said. "I've already called Lennox."

Zach felt the air whoosh right out of his lungs, which made speaking difficult. "Wow," came out a little strangled.

"So what do you think?"

Zach thought he'd like to see her. Watch that coyness he heard in her voice spread across her face. Kiss her as he said, "Sure, I think that would be fun." He started cleaning up again, a low laugh coming from his throat.

"Great," she said. "I think it'll be fun too." Their call ended, and Zach finished up in the barn. The trek back to the house only took a few minutes, because he practically ran to get out of the snow and the cold.

"Come on, Mother Nature," he complained as he went up the steps two at a time. He burst into the house to the scent of coffee and paused. "Hello?"

"Dad, it's just me," a man called, and Zach's heart burst with joy.

"Paul?" He closed the door behind him and the dogs and took a couple of steps before his son came out of the utility room. He looked good, with a lot of facial hair and a bright light in his eyes. Zach hurried over to him and enveloped him in a hug. "What are you doing here?"

He stepped back, sure his son was a mirage. He hadn't seen him since Christmastime. "How did you make it through the snow?"

"My truck can go through anything." Paul grinned at him, knowing that his mother did not like the truck. Zach had given him the money for a vehicle and told him to pick out one he liked, but he supposed the huge wheels were a little obnoxious.

"I forgot about that beast," he said. "I'm surprised I didn't hear you pull up."

Paul laughed and headed for the couch. "The semester is almost over, and we have three study days right now. Mom said I should come see you, so I'm here to see you."

"That's great," Zach said. "How's school going?"

"Meh," Paul said. "It's okay."

"You don't like it." Zach wasn't asking. He knew the value of a college education, and he knew what hard work could do too. He knew sometimes a person had to muddle through something they didn't like to have a future they did.

"I knew I wouldn't like it," Paul said. "But I'm not wasting your money, Dad. I go to class, and I study. Sometimes." He grinned, because that was so Paul. He'd always been the kid in the tree, out on the baseball field, jumping from the bridge over the river.

Zach had always said they'd have to tie him to a chair to get him to stay in school, but he hadn't used any ropes yet.

"How's the farm?" Paul asked.

"Great," Zach said. "Just great."

"Lindsey said to get as much dirt on your girlfriend as I could," Paul said next, absolute delight on his face.

"Oh, ho," Zach said, chuckling. "She did, huh?"

"That's right," Paul said. "And hey, I started dating someone new too, so we can swap stories."

Zach was sure his son's stories would be completely different than his, and he wasn't inclined to tell him about the trips to the senior citizen center or that he and Celia spent most of their time right there on the couch where he was sitting.

"You first," he said, leaning back into the couch. "Oh, and if you're hungry, a friend of mine sent home some leftovers. And I have cake."

"I saw the cake," Paul said. "And my girlfriend's name is Poppy."

"Poppy," Zach repeated. "And you're being safe with her, right, son?"

"Dad, come on," Paul said. "We've had the sex talk."

"I know, I know." Zach grinned at his son. "It's so good to see you. Talk to you in person."

"I guess I should've called or something. Mom said I could just show up."

"You can," Zach said. "Nothing going on here, though if you're still here on Tuesday, that's when *my* girlfriend comes to make lunch."

"She makes you lunch?"

"Yeah," Zach said. "She's my private chef too."

Paul's eyes nearly fell out of his head, and Zach laughed and laughed. He loved his kids, and he was so glad his son had come, even if it was only for a few days.

And he couldn't wait for Paul to meet Celia.

CHAPTER 11

Celia stopped in the middle of the road, her brothers' farm on her right and the Zuckerman's farm on the left. It seemed strange that something so thin could keep the families apart.

She knew water rights had caused problems before, but she felt like it was time to put this feud to rest. For good.

"Help us all," she prayed as she turned right and started down the lane toward the house where she'd grown up. Mack lived here now, and Lennox lived in the house on the right side of the lane. He'd built it with his own two hands during the months leading up to his wedding, and Ophelia was one of Celia's favorite people.

But she wasn't there to see her sister-in-law. She'd asked Mack and Lennox to be at the homestead that day, and she'd promised them an "amazing lunch" if they'd give her an hour of their time.

She carried in the grocery bags of buns, condiments, and other ingredients. Mack had a good grill pan she'd given him for Christmas a couple of years ago, and she'd have fresh, hot hamburgers on the table before her brothers came in from the farm.

"Larissa," she called as she went through the front door. "It's just me, Celia." She went into the kitchen, but she didn't see Mack's wife. She sometimes volunteered at the library, and she had a part-time job at the bakery in town.

She set about seasoning the beef and cutting tomatoes and onions for the toppings. She hummed a hymn to herself, a constant prayer in her mind to help her talk to her brothers about the Zuckermans.

Mack came in the back door with loud stomping and said, "Wow, there's so much snow out here."

"Ridiculous, isn't it?" she asked.

"Hey, sis." Mack grinned at her and stepped over to the kitchen sink to wash his hands. Then he hugged Celia. "Lennox is a few minutes behind me."

"Where's Larissa?"

"Uh, she went to her mother's." Mack looked away quickly, but Celia saw it.

Concern spiked through her, but her throat felt stuffed full of words. "She went to visit her mother? Or she went to her mother's?" Celia mixed together mustard and ketchup to make an orange sauce she knew Lennox particularly enjoyed. That way, she wouldn't have to look at her brother, something Mack would appreciate.

"I'm not sure," he said with a sigh.

"Where's Claire?"

"School," Mack said.

"So she's still here."

"Yes."

Celia looked up and met her brother's eye. "I'm so sorry."

Mack's jaw clenched, and his eyes filled with tears. "Me too."

"Is…Larissa okay?"

"She stopped going to therapy," he said. "Things have been getting worse for a while. I told her to do what she needs to do to be happy." He turned away from Celia. "I didn't think that meant cutting me and Claire out of her life."

"And the other kids?"

"They're doing okay," Mack said. "Still in college. They say they talk to her."

"Do you talk to her?"

"Yes," Mack said.

"So maybe things will work out," Celia said.

"Maybe," Mack said, wiping his hand across his face as he turned back to her. "I love her, and I can't stop loving her. I just want her to come home."

Celia abandoned her work at the island. "I know, Mack." She wrapped him in a hug, and everything ached for her older brother. "I know."

Mack held her tight for several long seconds and then stepped back. "I'm just getting through one day at a time."

"That's all any of us can do," she said. "I'll pray for you."

The back door opened again, and Lennox entered, along with a blast of cold air. "There he is," Celia said, glancing at Mack to find her older brother's mask back in place. Of course, Lennox knew about Larissa's departure. He lived just down the road, on the same land. Ophelia was probably feeding Mack and Claire every night.

"You should've told me," she said to him, knowing he'd understand without more details.

"Yeah? Like you told me you were dating again?"

"What?" Lennox splashed water on Celia he spun so fast from the sink. "You're dating again? Who?"

"Yeah," Mack said. "Who?"

Celia's heart floundered in her chest. Mack knew who she'd been spending her time with. "That's why I wanted you guys to come to lunch today," she said calmly. "I started dating Zach Zuckerman several weeks ago."

"Are you kidding me?" Lennox looked back and forth between her and Mack. "And you knew?"

"I heard a rumor," Mack said. "And I don't listen to too many rumors."

"Well, I'm standing here saying it's true. I really like him, and we get along great." Celia tapped the plates. "Let's eat while we talk. I want to know all about this feud between our two families."

"Oh, that's a boring story," Lennox said, collecting a plate and starting to load one of everything on his hamburger. "Water rights they said we stole, but we bought them, same as everyone else in the county."

"I know all about that," she said.

"Then you know what they're mad about."

"The newspaper article said they wanted to buy the extra acres jointly." She joined her brothers in making lunch. "Why didn't we let them?"

"That's a question for a ghost," Mack said.

Frustration filled Celia. "So we'll never know."

"And there's nothing we can do," Lennox said. "I've been across the street...I don't even know how many times. I took Owen a wedding gift when he and Aleah got married. Every time they had a baby, Ophelia made them dinner. I leave presents on their doorstep at Christmas." He shook his head. "That is one angry man."

"So there's no hope," Celia said.

"Hey, I don't care if you date Zach," Mack said. "I think it's pretty great, actually." He nudged Celia with his elbow. "Like this burger."

"What made you want to start dating again?" Lennox asked, just before taking a huge bite of his burger.

"I'm lonely," Celia admitted. "And I saw my friend find someone and get married—"

"Amanda Whittaker," Mack said.

"And I thought maybe I should try to find someone again," she said. "It's been nice, not sitting home alone with just Grizz, knitting."

"Oh, I don't even want to know what you're doing

with Zach in the evenings." Mack laughed, but Lennox just watched Celia.

"It's not us you'll have a problem with, sis," he said after he finally swallowed. "It's Owen Zuckerman."

Celia nodded, because she knew her brother was right, and she had no idea what to do about it.

🐍

CELIA FELT like she was on a violent roller coaster that just kept going up and down, down and up. Round and round. First the conversation with her brothers yesterday. And now lunch with Zach's son today.

Zach had texted to say he'd gone to the grocery store and had all of the ingredients, and he just needed her to put everything together into something delicious.

She pulled onto the road that led to Saltgrass Farm, glad the garage was already open, and she could drive right in. Before she could even get out of the car, the door opened, and Zach came out.

Opening the door, she stood and received his embrace. "Hey," she said with a laugh. "I guess you're as nervous as I am."

"A little," he admitted. "I don't see my kids a whole lot, and it's been so fun to have Paul here."

"I can't wait to meet him." Celia smiled up at Zach, and it felt like it would be the most natural thing in the world to kiss him. Time paused for a moment, and then he stepped back, a flush moving into his face.

Maybe he was thinking the same thing as her. She followed him inside, glad when he took her hand just inside the house. "Paul," he said. "This is my girlfriend, Celia Armstrong."

His son rose from the table, where he'd been looking at his phone. He looked so much like his father, with different pieces from Zach's ex-wife, obviously.

"Celia," he repeated, a smile spreading across his face. "It's good to meet you." He came forward and extended his hand toward her.

Celia shook it, joy moving through her. Such a feeling of love and a sense of home permeated this house, and she basked in it. "So good to meet you. Your father speaks of you often."

"Oh, great," Paul said with a laugh and a look toward his dad. "I'm sure that's not good."

"It is," Zach said. "Only good stuff." He went into the kitchen, and Celia followed him.

"All right, boys," she said. "What are we having for lunch today?"

"I told him you made the most amazing potato salad," Zach said.

"And he said that went so well with sloppy Joes," Paul added.

Celia nodded and turned to Zach's fridge. "I see how it is. You guys have this scripted."

Zach started to laugh, with Paul joining in. They sounded so similar, and Celia missed her daughters more in that moment than she had in a while. She'd been talking with Reagan more often, and her boyfriend had one more final interview before a date would be set.

Celia couldn't wait to hear what Dale and Reagan would decide to do. Reagan had already been looking at dresses, and she thought the shopping would go quickly once they had a date.

"Paul, what are you studying in school?" Celia asked.

"Engineering," he said. "But I think I'm going to switch to computer science."

"Oh, that's a big field right now," Celia said. "The men I work for own Springside Energy, and they code robots and stuff to find the natural gas."

"Really?" Paul came over to the bar and sat down. "That's so cool. I love robotics. I was in the robotics club in high school."

Celia smiled at him as she started peeling potatoes. "Why choose engineering then?"

"You know what? I don't know."

"You're young," Zach said. "Switch if you want."

"I probably will in the fall," Paul said. "Maybe Springside Energy has internships or something I can do this summer."

"I can talk to Graham," Celia said. She nodded to the pot. "Zach, will you fill that with hot water and put it on the stove?"

"Sure thing." He did as she asked, and it was wonderful to be in the kitchen with him, working together, with his son nearby. It almost felt like a family, and Celia wanted this moment to become her reality so, so badly.

She peeled and cut, boiled and mixed, and an hour later, she sat down with Zach and Paul for lunch. The conversation was easy, and she loved listening to Zach tell stories of his kids from his younger days.

Celia laughed, and she held Zach's hand, and everything felt so right. Paul's phone rang, and he said, "I'll be right back."

"I can see the name on that," Zach called after his son. Paul just laughed as he went down the hall toward the guest bedrooms.

"What was the name?" she asked.

"Anne," Zach said. "But when he got here, he told me his girlfriend's name was Poppy."

"Oh-ho," Celia said, still laughing. "There's so many stories here."

"Oh, there are." He brought her closer. "But first, I want to hear about your lunch with your brothers."

Celia snuggled into his side and allowed the warmth from his body to flow through hers. She hadn't had such strong feelings for a man in a long time, and she sure did like them. She liked that she wasn't home alone, and that she hadn't knitted in weeks.

"My family is fine with us dating," she said. "It'll be Owen we have to convince." She went on to tell Zach about Lennox taking gifts across the street, and Zach shook his head.

"I can't believe that."

"You can't believe Lennox took them gifts? Or that Owen wouldn't receive them?"

"A little of both, actually," he said. "My brother is very stubborn." But to refuse Christmas gifts? Zach wasn't sure.

"Oh, I've seen some of that Zuckerman stubbornness," she teased.

"You think so?" Zach kneaded her upper arm, and a wild streak moved through Celia. She turned to look up at him, sure he would close the distance between them and kiss her. She pulled in a long breath in preparation.

"Celia," he whispered. His eyes dropped to her mouth, his desire clear.

"Yes?"

"I am not stubborn."

She giggled as Zach swept his cowboy hat off his head, a clear preparation to kiss her. Everything in Celia started to tingle.

He lowered his head....

"Dad," Paul said, rushing back into the room. "That was my friend Anne, and her dog had her puppies."

Zach practically catapulted from the couch, jostling Celia in the process. The heat from her body filled her whole face, and she turned away from Paul. She stood up and straightened her clothes, almost desperate to leave. Embarrassment filled her as she started cleaning up lunch while Paul and Zach talked about the goldendoodle puppies.

"Just tell me how much," Zach said, and Celia smiled

to herself as she put a lid on the potato salad and put it in his fridge. Zach loved dogs and horses, but mostly dogs.

She glanced over to where his lay by the sliding glass door, flopped down on the floor, asleep. She often brought Grizz with her to Zach's, but she hadn't brought her pup today.

With the kitchen clean, and Zach and Paul still going strong about the puppies, Celia stepped over to Zach and slipped her hand into his. "I'm going to head out."

"You are?" He looked at her, surprise on his face.

"Yeah, you're here with your son." She put a big smile on her face and tipped up onto her toes to sweep a kiss across his cheek. He leaned into the touch, and a rush of satisfaction moved through Celia.

He wanted to kiss her too.

Maybe when his son left town, she could make that fantasy a reality.

CHAPTER 12

Z ach walked down the snow-packed lane, this one almost as familiar as his. He'd worked Finn's farm enough to be comfortable among the barns and stables, even if they were in the wrong places.

He fed the chickens, all five dogs waiting patiently outside the door of the henhouse. He checked the heat lamps, and everything seemed to be fine for the birds.

Finn hadn't left town, but Amanda's son had adopted another baby, and they'd gone to stay with Eli and Meg for a few days. Finn claimed there wasn't anything so magical as being a grandfather, and Zach could only take his word for it.

"Come on, guys," he said to the canines, glad he had them for company out here. Finn's farm sat on the outer outskirts of town, and Zach felt like no one could possibly hear him if he needed help. His farm was right in town, with neighbors on both sides, and even then, he felt somewhat isolated.

Finn's racehorses were doing just fine too, and Zach got them all fed and watered for the day, checked with the groom to make sure they'd get out of their stalls, and wiped the sweat from beneath his hatband.

Working two farms took a lot of hours, and he was glad his son had left the previous day. Celia wouldn't be coming until Saturday, as she was up at Whiskey Mountain Lodge, cooking up a storm for the Whittakers as they celebrated the new baby.

She'd invited him to the lodge on Sunday, and a river of nerves flowed through Zach. He wanted to go—and he would—but there would be a lot of people looking at him. Sizing him up. Making a judgement on whether they thought he was good enough for Celia—someone they'd known for a long time and loved.

His stomach growled by the time he finished the chores at Finn's farm, and he swung by a drive-through for a mushroom and Swiss burger before returning to his own place. The scent of Celia's perfume hung in the air, though she hadn't been there for twenty-four hours.

He glanced to the couch where he'd been a moment away from kissing her, and his imagination sprang to life. He didn't want to wait until Saturday to kiss her. And he certainly couldn't do it at the lodge on Sunday.

While he ate, he tapped out a quick message to Celia. *Can I bring you guys dinner tonight?*

As soon as he sent the text, a rush of stupidity ran through him. The reason she wouldn't be coming back to Dog Valley until Saturday was because she was cooking for the Whittaker family. She didn't need him to bring more food.

I mean, never mind, he sent quickly, his brain trying to find something else to say. *Are you staying at the lodge tonight? Maybe I can bring you dessert or something after a long day in the kitchen.*

What he really wanted to do, he couldn't say. But he wanted to see her, and he felt confident that the next time he did, he could kiss her.

I would love a peanut butter attack from Sweets. Her text made him smile, and even his food didn't distract him as he texted her back.

Done. What time would work?

I'm not staying at the lodge. My place. Seven-thirty?

Her place—somewhere he hadn't been yet. His heart pounded as he typed out three letters—*yes*—and went back to his lunch.

The hours between lunch and seven-thirty disappeared like smoke, and before Zach knew it, he had two huge ice cream shakes in the cupholder beside him as he navigated the quiet streets of Coral Canyon.

Her house came into view, and it was a normal, red-brick structure at the end of the block. He wasn't sure what he'd been expecting, but this wasn't it. She'd placed a wreath of bright, spring flowers on the door, probably an omen of hope that this long winter would end.

After turning into the driveway, he took his time gathering the ice cream before he stepped into the darkness. Her front door opened before he could knock, and she said, "Bless you," as she took her ice cream from him.

"Long day?" he asked with a chuckle, following her right inside her house. It felt like everyone inhaled and held their breath, including Grizz, the house, the town, the state, the universe.

He looked around, again not sure what he expected to find. Dozens of pictures of Brandon? A house frozen in time as she mourned the loss of her first husband? A mess? The furniture from her parents' house?

What he saw was a living room on his left that was tastefully decorated, an upright piano against the far wall. Did she play? How had he not known that?

Behind the couch, the house expanded into a dining room and a kitchen, and yes, there was one family picture, obviously taken years ago, of Celia, Brandon, and their two little girls.

"Come in," she said. "It's freezing outside."

Zach hastened to close the door behind him, embarrassed that he'd frozen and then started staring. He passed a hallway on his right that clearly went down to bedrooms and bathrooms, and a set of steps went down to a basement from the far end of the dining room.

"Do you play the piano?" he asked.

"Yes," she said. "I taught both of my girls too. A few other children right after Brandon died, and I was trying to figure out how to pay bills." She flashed him a smile, and he realized it was one of the only times they'd talked about her late husband.

His once-best friend.

"Cooking turned out to be more profitable," she said. "And I didn't have to get up at five-thirty in the morning to do it, or work after school when the girls were home."

He nodded, glad she'd found something she liked that she could use to support herself. At the same time, something very male inside him wanted to take care of everything for her.

"This is a nice place," he said.

"Thank you." She handed him a couple of paper towels and added, "I want to sit in the living room and relax."

Zach wanted that too. She did look tired, and his fantasies about kissing her started to wither. Quickly, before they could truly go, he said, "Can I hold that for a second?" He took her shake before she could protest and set it on the counter with his. "It's good to see you."

He gathered her in his arms, glad she came so easily and so willingly. His heartbeat skipped around, landing in weird places. "I think we got interrupted yesterday."

"We did?"

Zach didn't see what could possibly interrupt them here, but he swept his cowboy hat off his head and pulled back from her a little. "Yeah. You have to know I was about to kiss you yesterday."

A smile touched that beautiful mouth, and Celia

ducked her head. Zach touched his lips to her forehead, encouraged when she leaned into the pressure. He moved his mouth to her cheekbone, and slid it over to her ear. Her hands slipped across his shoulders, sending sparks down his spine and into his hair.

Every touch flamed with electricity, and Zach kissed a spot on her jaw before hesitating for one last moment.

With his eyes drifting closed, he barely touched his lips to hers, expecting a shower of fireworks—and getting them. He hadn't kissed a woman in a long, long time, and all he could do was hope he did it correctly.

By the way Celia pressed into him and kissed him back, Zach thought he did.

⁂

A COUPLE OF HOURS LATER, he pulled himself from her couch with the words, "I should go, sweetheart."

She moaned and held onto his hand. "Just stay a little longer." She'd said that twenty minutes ago too, and Zach had stayed. Number one, it had been a while since someone had wanted him to stay, and number two, he could sleep when he was dead.

But he didn't want to die that night on the drive back to Dog Valley, so he leaned toward her and kissed her again. There had been a lot of kissing after he'd landed that first one well enough, but she no longer tasted like peanut butter and chocolate.

She'd made coffee, and he'd asked her to play the piano

for him, and she'd detailed more about Reagan's upcoming wedding plans. Dale hadn't gotten the job in Texas, and he'd narrowed it down to two companies—one in California and one in Ohio. As soon as a decision was made, a date would be set, and Celia would be off to the races with planning.

"I should really go," he whispered against her lips. "I have two farms to take care of in the morning." And he'd be driving back and forth, because he couldn't make any of the animals wait for breakfast, not when he'd practically rushed through their dinnertime so he could bring Celia ice cream.

She kissed him, which kept him right where he was on her couch. He obliged, because wow, kissing Celia made everything inside him come alive. All the pieces that had been dark for so long glowed with life, and he experienced a joy he'd thought he never would again.

"All right," she finally said, her voice more like a sigh. "I'll see you Saturday."

"I can bring you something tomorrow night, too," he said. "Have you been to that new cookie place? They even deliver."

"Surprise me," she said with a smile, and Zach stood up. Grizz lifted his head, but he didn't move from the spot at the end of the couch. Zach gave the puppy a pat and headed for the front door.

"Seven-thirty again?" he asked, turning back to Celia.

"For now," she said. "I'll text you if something changes."

He nodded and went out into the freezing cold, though it was mildly warmer than before. The drive back to Dog Valley felt long and lonely, and Zach hated every minute of it.

He worked fast and furious the next morning, getting everything done around both farms as quickly as he could so he could once again drive to Coral Canyon to see his girlfriend. He whistled while he worked, his steps light and the tasks easy.

He knew why. Celia was why. He started thinking about her at the farm, waiting for him when he returned from his work with the animals. And in the summer and fall, she'd be there with cold lemonade and turkey sandwiches after he came in from the fields.

Slow down, cowboy, he told himself. He'd just kissed her. He hadn't proposed.

Did he even want to propose?

If he wanted her living with him in the farmhouse, then yes, he did. A warm, peaceful feeling filled him, and he beamed up into the bright sun. Mother Nature was cooperating—and he had another date with Celia that night.

It felt to Zach that nothing could go wrong, and he paused for a moment outside the goat shed.

In moments like these, he wanted to give glory to God, so he tipped his head down, touching the brim of his hat as he said, "Thank you, Lord." And since he'd lived fifty years on the Earth, he added, "And we don't need to go introducing some bad things now, to make me question everything, okay?"

And while God was not in the business of making deals with Zach Zuckerman, Zach still said, "Okay," anyway.

CHAPTER 13

C elia gazed down at the beautiful baby in her arms, a few stolen minutes away from the kitchen exactly what she needed this afternoon. Meg needed a nap, and she'd gone upstairs to find a spare bedroom to take one. Eli had taken Avery and Stockton down the road to Graham's and Laney's place, and Beau and Lily had gone down to Vi's house to take her some of the lunch Celia had made.

Silence pressed upon the lodge, and it was wonderful and cleansing. Celia had plenty to do in the kitchen still, from cleaning up after lunch to setting dinner in the oven. But she could hold this infant for a few more minutes.

Maybe forever.

The birth mother had chosen Eli and Meg suddenly and unexpectedly. But Amanda had arrived on the scene, and she'd taken Finn shopping for everything her son needed to bring the baby home while they'd driven to Butte to get him.

They'd named him Isaiah, and the old-fashioned name seemed to suit him just fine. He gurgled and groaned in her arms, and Celia shushed him while she patted his bottom. He settled right back to sleep, everything about this six-day old baby absolutely perfect.

Of course, he wasn't perfect, and the road ahead of him was long. His mother had been a drug addict, and while she'd cleaned up the last few months of her pregnancy, Isaiah still had some issues to deal with.

But for now, Celia rocked him, a nursery rhyme humming in the back of her throat. Her eyes drifted closed, and she thought about Zach. They obviously wouldn't have any children together, but they could have grandchildren.

A family.

Celia loved her daughters, and they'd been all the family she'd needed—until very recently. She tasted Zach on her lips again, and it was so very exciting to be in a relationship with a man again.

He'd kissed her like he adored her, which felt a little strange to Celia. She'd been working and problem-solving on her own for so long. She did what she wanted, when she wanted. To loop someone else in, find time for them, and think about them before herself was new and exciting, but also a shift in her routine.

Her phone buzzed, and she hastened to pick it up before it woke Isaiah. Her daughter's name sat on the screen, and she swiped her thumb across the device to answer the call.

"Reagan," she whispered into the phone. "I'm holding a sleeping baby."

"Wow, Mom," her daughter said. "That's amazing."

"He is amazing."

"Whose baby?"

"Eli Whittaker just adopted."

"That's so great."

It was great, but Celia knew it wasn't why her daughter had called. "What did you and Dale decide to do?"

"Ohio," Reagan said, all the excitement in the world in those three syllables. "It's a great company, and a good job, and he can start June first."

"Oh, that's sooner than you thought," Celia said, bracing herself for Reagan to say something crazy. Something like she wanted to get married before they left for Ohio.

"I've been looking at dresses, Mom," Reagan said, sending darts right through Celia's heart.

"And you want to get married before you move."

"I mean…yes."

Of course she did. Celia smiled, because Reagan loved Dale, and Dale adored Reagan, and they wouldn't want to be apart as this new chapter started in their lives.

"That's two months, Reagan," Celia said. "Are you going to come home to do it? Or do I need to start researching stuff in Cheyenne?"

"We'll come up there," she said. "I don't care about the wedding, Mom. I just want it to be simple."

"You're not Ruth," Celia said slowly. "But you do care about the wedding."

Her daughter sighed, and Celia wished they were in the same room having this conversation. Sometimes so much was lost, even over the phone.

"Do you want a reception center?" Celia asked. "Or should we have it at the church?"

"I don't know."

"Reagan," Celia said. "This isn't my wedding." She could plan it, sure. Buy the flowers and start sketching the cake design. But she didn't want to be responsible for something her daughter wouldn't like.

"Can I take a couple of days to think about it?"

"What have you been doing for the past few months?" Celia didn't mean to sound so harsh. But Reagan had known she'd marry Dale for a long time now.

Reagan sighed. "Honestly, Mom, we don't care. We just want to get married. I'd go to City Hall and do it, but you're not here."

"Don't you dare do that," Celia said, true fear pinning her heart against her ribcage. "It's bad enough your dad —" She cut herself off, her lungs seizing at the thought that Brandon would not be there for his daughter's wedding.

Of course he wouldn't. She'd known that for a long, long time.

She cleared her throat. "Have you thought about who will walk you down the aisle?"

"Dale's brother," Reagan whispered. "Rushton said he'd do it."

Celia nodded though her daughter wasn't there to see it. "We could have the wedding at the lodge," she said. "There's a huge backyard here, and we could get tents and chairs and everything." It would be so much nicer than Amanda's wedding in the cramped living room.

"That's fine, Mom. Those kinds of things I don't care about."

"What about the cake?"

"You're making the cake."

"Do you have a design in mind?" Celia watched Isaiah sleep, wishing she could grasp onto the peace she'd experienced only a few minutes ago.

"A design?"

"Yes, dear," Celia said as patiently as she could. "Cakes have designs. Two tiers. Three. Four. Seven. Colors. Traditional. Flowers."

"Oh, um...."

Celia laughed, the sound coming out before she could censor it. The baby in her arms squirmed again, his newborn eyes coming open for a moment. He scrunched up his face and wailed, and Celia held the phone to her ear with her shoulder so she could quiet him.

With Isaiah subdued and her laugher subsided, she said, "How about this? How about I put together some options and you choose?"

"That would be great, Mom." Reagan's relief came through the line loud and clear. "And you're still coming to graduation, right?"

"Of course I am," Celia said. "I would never miss my baby girl's college graduation."

"You can bring Zach."

"Good," Celia said. "Because I probably will."

"Oh, so things are serious with him." Reagan didn't make it into a question.

"I would say...yes," Celia said, thinking of the kisses they'd shared. She didn't go around kissing everyone, but she also wasn't sure she'd met her second soulmate already. Amanda had dated a lot of men before she and Finn had fallen in love and gotten married. Zach was Celia's very first boyfriend in many years. Maybe she should be dating more people.

But the very idea made her recoil away from the thought of dating at all. She didn't want to be juggling her job here as well as more than one man. She could barely keep up with Zach as it was.

"That's so great, Mom," Reagan said. "I can't wait to meet him."

"I'll talk to you soon," she said as Isaiah started to cry again. "I'll email you the cake designs."

"Love you," Reagan said over the wails, and Celia called the sentiment back before she hung up. She stood, bouncing Isaiah now.

"Oh, are you hungry? Are you?" She took the fussy baby into the kitchen and started preparing a bottle for him. As she worked and then settled back into the rocking recliner to feed Isaiah, she let herself think through several options for Reagan's wedding. She'd put those together this afternoon and get them emailed off.

She needed to make a few phone calls, especially if they needed to book a venue, and she needed to remind Zach about the trip to Cheyenne for Reagan's graduation. He'd meet Ruth then too, as she went to college at the University of Wyoming also.

Her heartbeat skittered through her, but she gazed down at Isaiah as he steadily sucked down his afternoon feeding, and all the peace and love she'd felt for him earlier returned.

"You're just the best boy, aren't you?" she whispered to him, taking the comfort in that moment, because she knew it wouldn't last for long.

※

WHEN HER DOORBELL rang that night, Celia's heartbeat fluttered in her chest. She glanced at the clock, confused, and then realized it was seven-thirty.

"Zach." She hurried to stand, sending her chair scraping along the tile in her dining room. The table was covered with papers and notes, her laptop, and her half-eaten dinner. She'd been so engrossed in chatting with Reagan and coming up with plans and ideas, that she hadn't even been able to finish the pasta casserole she'd made by the gallon.

She'd left half of it up at Whiskey Mountain Lodge, of course, where Graham and Beau would eat it, and the other half at Amanda's house here in town, where Andrew, Amanda, and Eli would be grateful for the food.

"Hey," she said, her voice breathless as she pulled open the door to find Zach standing there with a long, pink box in one hand and dozens of red roses in the other.

"Hey, gorgeous," he said, his voice sexy and strong. His eyes glittered at her from underneath that delicious hat, and she didn't step back when he entered the house. She did close the door behind him before she tipped up onto her toes and took his face in both of her hands.

He chuckled as she kissed him, his hands full so he couldn't hold her properly. "Let me set this stuff down."

"Oh, I'll take those flowers," she said. He handed them to her, and a rush of affection overcame her. She glanced at him, heat filling her from top to bottom. "You're so thoughtful. I love roses."

"I know," he said. "You told me once before."

And he'd remembered. She linked her arm through his and went into the kitchen with him. As she pulled a vase from the cupboard above the fridge, she said, "Reagan wants to get married before she and Dale move to Ohio." She pulled the rubber band off the stems. "By June first."

"Wow."

"Two months," Celia said. "We've been going back and forth on some plans." She nodded toward the dining room table, where she could see the green stripe across the top of her chatbox, indicating her daughter had sent her a couple of new messages. "Are you still good to come to Cheyenne with me for her graduation?"

"Yep," Zach said, coming around the island and sweeping one hand along her waist.

Shockwaves moved through Celia's body, and she abandoned her flower arranging to kiss her boyfriend. She practically melted into him, no matter how much she told herself not to. He was strong, and tall, and handsome, and he seemed to know how to kiss her in such a way that made her feel desired.

Celia had been needed in the past. Of course she had. Her kids needed her. Graham Whittaker had needed her.

But Zach *wanted* her. She could feel it in his very touch, in the slow way he explored her mouth, hear it in the growl in the back of his throat.

By the time he pulled away, Celia felt lightheaded and weak, and she leaned against the counter to finish getting the roses in the vase. That done, she turned toward the treat he'd brought. "I've never had Crumb cookies before."

"They're fantastic," he said. "And they were warm when I got them." He opened the pink box to reveal four super-sized cookies inside. "I got the signature chocolate chip, of course." He gazed down into the box like it was full of gold. "But the snickerdoodle are my favorite." Picking one of those up, he took a bite. He tipped his hatted head back and groaned. "Oh, yeah."

Celia laughed at him, glad something as simple as snickerdoodles could make him so happy. After all, she had a great snickerdoodle recipe, and she could make huge cookies too.

A cookie bar. The idea popped into her head, and she took her treat over to the dining room table. Reagan loved cookies too, and as she typed out the idea for the reception following the wedding, Celia was so grateful Zach had brought her the idea.

And the cookies.

And himself.

Fine, she was grateful for a whole lot about the cowboy who'd come over to sit by her. She grinned at him, and he grinned back, and all of her doubts about not dating enough disappeared.

Maybe she didn't need to be Amanda and date a lot of different people. Maybe she'd be lucky enough to find her Prince Charming on her first try.

CHAPTER 14

Zach folded another pair of slacks, careful to keep the crease exactly straight, and placed the pants in his suitcase. The past few weeks with Celia had only proven to him how isolated and lonely he'd become at Saltgrass Farm.

When she wasn't there, he wished she was. When she was, the only thing he could feel was joy. He'd been in love before, but it had been a long time, and with only two months of dating under his belt, he still wanted to take things slow.

They'd spent a lot of time around at various places in Dog Valley, as well as several restaurants in Coral Canyon. She seemed to have an affinity for activities at the senior center, as well as taking him to every romantic comedy that came to the theater in town.

He didn't mind either, because he got to see Celia. They were going to Cheyenne today. Their first road trip together, and Zach would be lying if he said he wasn't nervous. As he zipped his suitcase closed, his heart skipped a beat. Maybe two.

He was driving, though the roads were clear now and the snow had been melting in earnest since April started. It was as if Mother Nature had flipped a switch and turned off the bad weather.

Zach had been enjoying the better weather, but everything on Saltgrass Farm seemed made of mud. He was glad he'd be away for a few days, and he'd helped Finn enough that he didn't feel bad asking his best friend to feed his animals.

An alarm went off, and Zach flew into motion. "All right, guys," he said to the dogs as he entered the living room. "Finn will be here in a few hours to take you back to his place. Be nice to his Labs, okay?"

He scrubbed Ginger and then Maple as they grinned their happy smiles at him. They sat on the bench looking out the back windows, their favorite spot as the sun warmed the day. Maple licked his hand, and Zach chuckled. "I have to go. Picking up Celia soon."

He put his suitcase in the back of his truck and headed out. The drive passed quickly, and when he pulled into Celia's driveway, another pickup truck sat there. He parked beside the fancy, red vehicle, eyeing it suspiciously.

His nerves tripled, and he didn't even know whose truck that was. "Probably Lennox," he muttered to himself as he pulled to a complete stop. He walked and rang the doorbell and waited.

The door got yanked open, and indeed, Lennox stood there. "Hello," he said, his eyes sliding down Zach's body and back to his face. "Celia, there's a man here for you." A smile twitched against his lips, and he finally extended his hand toward Zach.

"Good to see you, Zach."

"You too, Lennox." Relief spread through Zach as he shook Celia's brother's hand.

"Don't make him stand on the porch, Lenny." Celia arrived, wiping her hands on a kitchen towel. She grinned at Zach. "Come on in, Zach."

He entered, glad when Celia swept a kiss across his cheek right in front of her brother. "Mack's here too," she said. "I didn't know they were stopping by, and they're making me late." She increased the volume of her voice with each word, hitting the T on "late" extra-hard as she glared at Lennox.

He only laughed, something Zach probably would've done if he'd had any sisters. Zach couldn't help smiling, and he couldn't imagine the scene if Celia came over to his farm while his brothers were there.

It was actually a nightmare that woke him up sometimes.

"And there's Mack," Celia said, indicating the kitchen where Mack was cutting a sandwich in half. "I hate to throw you to the wolves, but I'm not done packing yet." She flashed him an apologetic look and hurried down the hall.

"Zach." Mack left the knife on the counter, thankfully, and came around to shake Zach's hand. "How are you?"

"Just fine," Zach said, catching himself before he added a "sir" to the end of the sentence. After all, Mack wasn't Celia's father. "How's your mother?"

"Oh, she's hanging in there." Mack exhaled, put a strained smile on his face, and returned to his sandwich.

"Coffee?" Lennox asked as if he owned the place. He got out a mug before Zach could answer, and he figured he could sip some coffee while Celia finished packing.

"So you're going to Cheyenne," Mack said.

"Yes," Zach said. He wasn't sure what else to say, so he just stood there. Lennox poured the coffee and nudged the mug closer to Zach.

He picked it up and reached for the sugar spoon.

"Seems serious, doesn't it, Lennox?" Mack asked as if Zach had left the room.

"Fairly serious," Lennox agreed. "Especially considering Celia hasn't dated anyone in so long." He sipped his coffee as Mack took a bite of his sandwich. Their voices sounded casual, but Zach felt like he was walking on live coals.

"I suppose," Zach said. "It's her daughter, and Reagan's important to her."

"Reagan and Ruth are everything to her," Mack said.

"I have two daughters, too," Zach said. "I understand the feeling." He sat down at the bar and put two spoonsful of sugar in his coffee. "And a son."

Lennox smiled at him. "How's your brother?"

The breath left Zach's body. "He's...about the same." He offered an apologetic smile and picked up his coffee.

"How's that going to work out?" Mack asked.

"I don't—"

"Ready," Celia said, arriving back in the kitchen. She exhaled and looked at the three of them. "You guys literally never stop by." She pushed a palm against Mack's shoulder. "Go back to the farm. I'm leaving for Reagan's graduation."

She met Zach's eye. "Are you ready?" Nerves lived in her expression, and he grinned to reassure her.

"So ready." He left his coffee mug on the counter, hoping Lennox would clean it up. He picked up Celia's bag and added, "I'll be in the truck," thinking she'd want a moment to talk to her brothers.

Sure enough, she stayed behind while he towed her suitcase out to the truck. He'd buckled his seatbelt and started the truck before she came outside. Once she was in, he backed out of the driveway to find both of her brothers standing in the doorway, watching them.

"They're nice," he said, his voice much too high.

"They're maddening," she said. "I'm so sorry. They just showed up, and I couldn't get them to leave."

"You could've texted." He cut her a look, a chuckle coming from his throat. "I'm not upset."

"They like you." Celia beamed back at him. "Lennox actually said he thinks it's great we're seeing each other."

"Really?"

"Yeah." She pulled out her phone and glanced at it. "And we're only a few minutes late leaving."

"We'll be fine," he said. They weren't leaving the state, but Cheyenne was still five and a half hours from Coral Canyon. They'd stop for lunch in two of those and have the rest of the afternoon to get there. They couldn't check in to their hotel until four anyway, and they had plenty of time.

"Tell me more about Reagan," Zach said, still so nervous to meet her daughters.

"She's bright," Celia said. "She'll size us up in about four seconds, so you're going to hold my hand, remember?"

"I always want to hold your hand," Zach said, grinning at her.

"She's the easy-going daughter," Celia said. "She likes a good party, and loud music, and plenty of candy."

"So she came from Brandon," he said. "As you don't really like any of those things."

"Hey," Celia protested. "I like a good party."

"As long as there aren't too many people there," he said.

A beat of silence passed before she started giggling. "Okay," she said between the laughter. "As long as there aren't too many people there." She quieted, and Zach loved the comfortable silence between them.

"She definitely came from Brandon," Celia said. "He was the fun parent, for sure. I was the one who made them eat vegetables and put their cereal bowl in the dishwasher."

"Heck, I barely do those two things," Zach said. He suddenly had the very real thought that he'd like Celia in his house, taking care of him. He'd even eat his vegetables.

"Ruth is a little bit more like me," Celia said. "She likes taking care of details, and she studies hard, and she's a little quieter." She smiled to herself, and Zach watched her more than the road in front of him.

Pulling himself together, he focused out the windshield and kept his thoughts away from how he might crash and burn in front of her two daughters later that evening.

HOURS LATER, they'd arrived in Cheyenne, checked in to their hotel, and he'd changed into one of those pairs of slacks he'd brought with him. Celia had just texted to say her daughters were downstairs, and Zach left his hotel room to find his girlfriend coming toward him.

"I'm so nervous," he said, deciding to just get his feelings out in the open.

"Relax," she said, slipping her hand through his arm. "They're going to love you."

"You think so?"

She beamed up at him, reaching up to touch the brim of his cowboy hat. "I mean, you're handsome, and kind, and sexy...." She let her voice hang there, and Zach leaned down to kiss her.

Her touch calmed him, and he lost himself in their kiss for a moment. He pulled away and leaned his forehead against hers, realizing he'd lost his cowboy hat at some point. "Celia," he whispered.

"Mm?"

"I think I'm falling for you."

She swayed with him, simply holding onto his shoulders like she needed him to stand. He wanted to dance with her through everything in his life.

"I really like you too," she finally whispered. "But my phone has buzzed about six times since we've been standing here." She cradled his face in both of her hands and gazed at him, so much adoration in her eyes that Zach almost got lost in them.

A quick elevator ride downstairs led them to the lobby, and he secured his hand in hers as they moved toward the revolving doors that marked the exit.

Two women stood from a couch, and Zach saw Celia in both of them immediately.

"Mom!" Reagan squealed as she launched herself at Celia, and Zach let go of her hand so she could hug her daughter.

He stood there, lost amidst all the laughing and hugging and exclaiming. Finally, Celia stepped back to his side and put her hand in his. He squeezed as she said, "Girls, this is my boyfriend, Zach Zuckerman." She smiled up at him, and Zach grinned down at her.

Then he extended his free hand toward Reagan. "Hello," he said. "I've heard so much about both of you."

Reagan's smile was bright and still on her face, but she was definitely appraising him, probably right down to the tonalities in his voice. She shook his hand and said, "Nice to meet you, Zach."

"And you." He faced Ruth, who also wore a smile. She was definitely much more like Celia, with hair almost the exact same shade and those big hazel eyes that Zach loved.

"Hello, Ruth," he said easily.

"Zach." She shook his hand too, and the two girls edged closer together, giggles coming from their mouths.

"Oh, come on, girls," Celia said. "Ray, where's Dale tonight?"

"He's in the car," she said. "Come on, he's probably about to get towed. You two took *forever* to come down."

"Yeah," Ruth said. "Were you upstairs making out or something?"

Zach coughed, heat flaming right into his face, while Celia laughed.

"Well," she said. "I haven't dated in a long time."

Zach wasn't sure what that meant, but her hand tightened in his as they all started moving toward the revolving doors. Zach felt like he'd passed a major test, and he could only hope that his daughters liked Celia when they finally met her.

CHAPTER 15

C elia kept her eyes on the speaker, annoyance surging through her. Zach had definitely passed the test of meeting her daughters—they adored him—but he'd been texting for a solid twenty minutes now.

Sure, she was bored too, especially as the twenty-something in front of the mic said something she didn't understand and the crowd started laughing. Well, the younger crowd, at least.

But he was the valedictorian, and she'd enjoyed most of what he'd said. Zach probably hadn't heard a word.

"Everything okay?" she asked, leaning over to see if she could catch a glimpse of who he was talking to. Her heart had been beating a little too loudly since the text-fest had begun, her worries over Owen finding out Zach had not ended his relationship with her always in the back of her mind.

"I have a little problem on the farm," he said, barely glancing at her. His eyes lifted, but they didn't meet hers before he moved them back to the device. "First I was talking to Finn, and now I'm texting Owen." He angled the phone toward her so she could see his brother's name at the top of the screen.

"He wants to know what I'm doing in Cheyenne." Tension radiated from Zach's powerful shoulders, and Celia hated that he was in this position.

"What's the problem on the farm?"

"Flooding." His thumbs moved quickly over the screen. "Owen and Xander are going up there now. They'll keep me updated." He pushed the power button on the side of his phone and stuck it in his breast pocket.

With a stretched smile, he lifted his arm around her shoulders and focused back up to the front of the huge arena, where the valedictorian was *still* talking.

"What did you tell them?" she whispered.

"Nothing." He pressed his lips to her forehead and kept his eyes on the student.

Celia's gut churned. But the valedictorian finally stopped talking, and applause filled the basketball arena. "Finally," she muttered as the Dean of Education got up and announced that they would now be reading the graduate names.

Armstrong was very soon in the alphabet, and pride filled her with every name that got called. When Reagan Fawn Armstrong was finally called, she whooped and clapped along with the people in her row.

Dale's parents sat down on the other end of the row, with several of his brothers and sisters there. Only she and Zach had made the trip for Reagan, as her mother was elderly, and her brothers had a farm to attend to.

But Dale's family was from Cheyenne, and she appreciated them all being here. Of course, their son was graduating too, but she met Vivian's eyes, noticing that the other woman was teared up too.

She couldn't believe her oldest daughter was now graduating from college. *Brandon,* she thought. *You would've loved to have been here.*

All of these big moments in her life—in her daughter's lives—were bittersweet. She was so glad and grateful that she could experience them. She'd never felt so much pride than when her daughters earned awards or trophies, wore special sashes at their graduations, or had something else to celebrate.

But those occasions also always reminded her that only half of the important people were there. Brandon couldn't attend, though as the names continued to be announced, she felt his presence with her. There for a moment, then gone. Almost like he didn't want to intrude on her life.

As soon as the ceremony concluded, Zach burst to his feet. "I need to call my brother real quick." He leaned down and kissed her briefly. "I'll meet you at the truck, okay?"

They'd driven themselves with Ruth, as Reagan had to arrive much earlier than them. She could barely nod before Zach was out in the aisle and taking the steps two at a time to get out before the crowd got too thick.

Celia watched him go, worry needling way down into her heart. She understood farm problems, having grown up on one. Adding in familial tension would only make things worse. She sent up a quick prayer for him, that he would know what to say and how, before she looped her arm through Ruth's and started much more slowly up the steps.

"Where did Zach go?" Ruth asked.

"Oh, he's got some flooding on his farm."

"And he lives up in Dog Valley, right?"

"Yes." Celia sighed, and Ruth leaned into her.

"You really like him, Mom." She whispered it, almost like Celia's affection for Zach was a secret.

"Yes," she whispered back, serious as she could be. "I really like him."

Ruth grinned at her, her eyes all-searching. "I'm so glad."

"You are? You don't think…I don't know. That I'm too old to be dating?"

"Why would I think that?"

Reagan would've laughed and bumped Celia with her hip. Ruth just watched her mom as they finally reached the top of the steps and moved to exit the stadium.

"You deserve to be happy, Mom. And he obviously makes you very happy."

"He does," she mused, wondering how deep her feelings for Zach went. Just last night he'd admitted he was falling in love with her. He hadn't used the word *love*, though, and she'd been careful not to as well.

But he kissed her like he was falling *in love* with her, and she kissed him back the same way. She enjoyed spending time with him, and she was disappointed when their plans fell through. He still hadn't met the Whittaker boys, as the Sunday he was supposed to come up to the lodge had dawned with pinkeye in abundance up the canyon. Little Ronnie had it, and so did Brayden, and everyone had stayed home after church.

"Well, I'm glad," Ruth said. They went outside, where they'd meet Reagan and Dale around the side of the arena, as they'd planned.

Celia tugged her jacket a little tighter against the breeze, surprised when Ruth stepped away from her and toward a man clearly waiting for her. She paused and stretched up to kiss him, and Celia pulled in a tight breath.

"Ruth."

Her daughter turned to face her, pure joy on her face. "Mom, I wanted you to meet someone."

"This man you just kissed, I'm assuming." She didn't like surprises, and Ruth didn't normally either. But she put a kind smile on her face and once again wished Brandon were there with her.

Or Zach.

One of them, so she'd have someone's arm to hold onto. To anchor her. Someone she could go through tumultuous things with and not be alone.

"Brandon, this is my mother, Celia."

She could barely breathe. "Brandon?"

"Yes," Ruth said, still lit up from the inside. "We've been seeing each other this semester. Mom, this is my boyfriend, Brandon Thompson."

He swept her into a hug, his smile genuine and his spirit good. Celia smiled and patted his shoulder. "So nice to meet you," she said. "And you didn't say *anything*." She laughed at her daughter, because keeping a boyfriend a secret was so like her.

"Well, Reagan's had a lot going on." Ruth shrugged. She'd always let her older sister overshadow her, and it made Celia's heartstrings sing.

"She certainly has." Celia grinned at both of them. "Will you be coming to the wedding, Brandon?" The name only stumbled out of her mouth for a moment.

"Yes, ma'am," he said, pulling Ruth tighter against his side. "We'll be there."

The wedding was still six weeks away—and Celia had so much to do before the day arrived—but the confidence in Brandon's voice suggested he really liked Ruth. No wonder she was practically glowing.

"Where did you two meet?" she asked as they all started walking again.

"Brandon is the TA in my—"

A shriek drowned out the last word in Ruth's sentence, as Reagan-the-Tasmanian-devil had spotted them. She grabbed onto Ruth and Celia at the same time, while trying to jump up and down.

The conversation paused as congratulations were said, hugs given, and cards exchanged. Dale lined up with his family, and Reagan snapped their picture with several cell phones.

"Where's Zach?" she asked at the same time Celia realized she'd have to be in a picture too—alone.

She didn't want to do this alone. She'd invited him specifically to be with her during times like this. And to meet her daughters, but still.

"He had a phone call," she said, feeling stupid. She pulled out her phone. "I'll call him and see where he is."

There were plenty of other pictures to take, and if he would pick up the line, maybe he could get back here for one with her and her daughters.

But he didn't answer. Not the first time, or the second.

Frustration and a bit of humiliation filled her, but she stood between Reagan and Dale and smiled like she'd just won an amazing award. She stood with Reagan alone, and grinned. She got a picture of just her and the girls.

They eventually all headed for the parking lot, and Celia still hadn't gotten a text or a call from Zach. He was tall enough though, that she could see him standing, his back to them, by the tailgate of his black truck, his phone still stuck to his ear.

"I'll call him," she heard him say from a few vehicles down. "Just hook it up, Owen. It'll be fine." Heavy annoyance carried in his voice, and Celia slowed her steps.

"I'm going to go with Brandon," Ruth said. "We'll meet you at the restaurant."

"Okay, dear," Celia said, barely registering that her daughter had left, and she was now alone to face Zach.

"I know it will flood his property," Zach said. "It's what happens every year. The dangers of living down the slope, you know?"

Celia arrived at his side, and he looked down at her. "Owen, I have to go. Just do it, and text me when it's done. I'll call Jonas." He hung up and looked away, a storm swirling on his face.

"You're going to flood Jonas's property?" She'd spent enough time at Saltgrass Farms to know Jonas Crenshaw was the neighbor to the west who owned all the land behind Zach's farm.

"We use his fields for runoff," Zach said, practically biting out the words.

"*You* use his fields for runoff." Celia wasn't sure why she was arguing with him, other than her own annoyance at him running off and leaving her had resurfaced. She walked between the cars to the passenger door. "The dangers of living downstream could be that you don't have access to your water rights anymore."

"What does that mean?" He came up behind her, and Celia turned to face him.

"Are we kidding ourselves?" she asked.

"Are we talking about the farm?"

She shook her head. "I don't know what we're talking about." A chill ran from the top of her head to the soles of her feet. "Can you open the truck? I'm cold."

He did, and he helped her climb onto the bench seat

too before closing the door and rounding the truck to get behind the wheel.

"Celia," he said. "I'm sorry. I…."

"You left me and missed the graduation pictures with my daughter."

Zach exhaled, his fingers tightening around the steering wheel. But he said nothing.

"And your family has been blaming mine for something very similar to what you just told your brother to do."

"No," he said, shaking his head.

"But your brothers will never be okay with us." Tears pricked her eyes. Why hadn't she acknowledged this truth before? Had she really clutched so tightly to a fool's hope?

"My brothers don't get to decide," he said quietly. "They don't live with me, and—"

"And what?" she interrupted. "We'll never spend holidays with them? You'll go visit your family's farm by yourself?"

"Yes." He twisted toward her. "Yes," he said more forcefully. "Okay? Yes. I'm not going to let my family history with yours ruin possibly the best thing I've got in my life."

Celia searched his face, trying to figure out what he'd said at the same time she tried to discover how she felt about it.

"And I didn't just do what our families have been feuding about for a century. Really just *my* family." He shook his head and started the truck. "My farm floods every year. I always drain onto Jonas's fields. Always. I just call him, and he usually comes and helps with the pipes."

He backed out of the parking space a little too fast, and Celia's heartbeat bobbed around in the back of her throat.

"Zach," she said.

He drove normally, but his fingers were in a fist around the steering wheel, almost like he could strangle it. "I'm sorry I missed the pictures. Maybe we can get some at the restaurant." His voice had lost the edge, and she wondered if he really had calmed so quickly.

Celia nodded though he wasn't looking at her. He navigated them through the streets of Cheyenne flawlessly, pulling into the crowded parking lot. As he reached for the door handle, still silent, Celia said, "Zach, wait."

He did, turning to look at her. He was dark and beautiful, stormy and dangerous, loving and kind, all at the same time.

She swallowed, gathering her courage. "I think you're the best thing in my life too."

CHAPTER 16

Zach's heart beat irregularly, Celia's words bouncing around inside his brain. A smile touched her mouth, and she ducked her head. "You don't need to stare at me like that."

Oh, but he did. He hadn't been the best thing in anyone's life in a long, long time. Sure, his kids loved him. His dogs. His horses.

But there was nothing like the love of a good woman.

Of course, she hadn't said she loved him. But Zach felt with enough time and enough work, their relationship could be something beautiful.

Instead of saying anything, he got out of the truck and hurried around it so he could be at her door when she slipped from the bench seat. He gathered her into his arms and kissed her, hoping his touch would say everything his vocal cords couldn't.

"JONAS?" Zach pushed open the barn door at the same time he called.

"In the office," Jonas called, and Zach went past the stalls, smiling at the few horses housed there. Jonas had a much bigger animal population on his farm, though it was only a few acres bigger than Zach's.

"Hey, so my brother said things went okay with the piping." Zach felt bad he wasn't here to help out, but only because he didn't want the burden to fall on his friend. He didn't miss tromping through the mud, or washing Ginger and Maple afterward because they refused to stay inside.

Thankfully, Finn had them when Owen and Xander had come up to take care of the flooding.

"It did." Jonas leaned back in his chair, smiling up at Zach. "Is the farm drying out?"

"Slowly," Zach said. He'd only been back in town for a day, and he'd only been out to feed once—that morning. "How are things here?"

"Going good. I got quite a bit of flooding too."

"Yeah, I saw it out there." Zach smiled at him. "Well, I just wanted to say thanks for helping. My brother...he was okay?"

"Oh, I know how Owen is." Jonas smiled again, his eyes a little harder now. "He was fine, and Xander sure knows how to talk."

"Does he?" Zach grinned. "I don't get down to see them much."

"He said that. Said you have a new girlfriend." The curiosity on his face matched that in his voice.

"Yeah." Zach reached up and took off his cowboy hat, his heart suddenly pumping extra-hard. "What else did they say?"

"Not much. Owen got real quiet after that, and we just got the work done."

"They don't like Celia," Zach said, giving voice to the truth for the first time.

"Why not? She seems great, and you're obviously over the moon for her. Don't they want you to be happy?"

Zach didn't know how to answer that. "Our families have a long-standing disagreement." He gave Jonas a sad smile and shrugged. "I'm hoping they'll come around."

"Martha and I will pray for you." He stood up and shook Zach's hand.

"Thanks, Jonas." Zach pulled his next-door neighbor into a quick hug. "You're sure everything is okay with the pipes?"

"Of course. We drain into that field every year." A measure of confusion moved across his face.

"Great, thanks." Zach wanted to get out of there before he had to answer any more questions. Celia had simply made him question whether what he'd done was okay or not. But it was. He and Jonas both drained their farms into the lower field. Just because Jonas owned it didn't mean Zach had done something wrong.

Back on his own farm, he started cleaning up as much

as he could, glad the pipes had been going for a couple of days now.

A week passed, and the farm dried out little by little. He put the horses out in the field, and they got busy eating the new grass. He spent some time online, looking at pigs and goats, thinking he might expand his farm a little bit.

His first love was horses, for sure. And dogs. He did have a few goats already, but his biggest herd was chickens. He loved eggs, and he sometimes went to the summer Farmer's Market to sell the extras he had.

In the end, he decided pigs would require too much extra work. Another pen. A barn. More food. And he didn't want to deal with the smell either. So he made a note to wait until the county fair came to town that fall, and he'd try to buy a few new goats from the 4-H kids.

Finally, everything worked out for him to join Celia up at Whiskey Mountain Lodge after church one Sunday. He was looking forward to an afternoon with her that he didn't normally get, and his phone sang as he got out of the shower.

Wet, and with the slippery floor, he didn't hurry to get it, and the call went to voicemail. He'd barely wrapped a towel around his waist when the phone rang again. He did bustle to get it this time, surprise and happiness bursting through him when he saw Celia's name on the screen.

"Hey, sweetheart," he drawled, already excited to see her later that day. Yes, they'd been spending time together during the week, but she'd been much busier, what with her daughter's wedding coming up. She hadn't stayed as long as she usually did, and he'd missed her presence in his life.

"Hey," she said. "How close to ready are you?"

"I just got out of the shower." He looked at himself in the mirror. He hadn't shaved in a while, and he had a nice beard going. Maybe he should keep it for a while. The hair often itched him, and he shaved it off when he couldn't stand it.

"I was wondering if you'd like to come to church with me."

Zach's pulse started shooting around his body. His mouth opened, but no sound came out.

"You'd have to leave in probably ten minutes," Celia said. "My church is a little earlier than yours. But then we could go up to the lodge together."

"Yes," Zach blurted, already moving to get dressed. "I'll be there. You want me to pick you up, or meet you?"

"Do you think you have time to pick me up?"

"I have no idea where your church is."

"It's across town. I'll text you the address. It's closer to the main highway, and you can meet me there."

"Okay," he said, pulling his slacks from the hanger in his closet. "I'll see you in a few minutes, then."

"All right. Bye." She sounded flirty and fun, and Zach couldn't wait to sit next to her on the bench. Hold her hand. Smell her perfume, and dream about kissing her later.

He dressed quickly, skipping his plans to shave. Grabbing a tie and his shoes, he practically jogged into the kitchen, where he hastened to feed the golden retrievers and get them fresh water.

"I'll be gone most of the day," he said. "But I'll throw you girls a ball when I get back, okay?" He couldn't stay up at the lodge all day and all night. He had animals to feed on the farm. But Celia had been wanting him to meet the Whittakers for weeks now. Illness and other family celebrations had kept him away, but not today.

Today, he was going to meet them all. Get to taste her cooking again. And kiss her. As Zach buckled his seatbelt, his tie looped loosely around his neck, he knew he was in love with Celia Armstrong.

He didn't dare admit it out loud, not even to himself. Not yet. But the feeling bubbled there, making him emotional as he put in the address and got going.

He arrived a bit late, but there were still a handful of people entering the church building. He tied his tie as he walked, tucking everything and making sure he looked presentable before he pulled open the door and went inside. Instantly, his stress decreased as a sense of wonder and awe overcame him.

Though he was already late, he took a moment to close his eyes and give a prayer of gratitude to God. For the ability to center himself in the gospel. For Celia. For his farm, his friends, his family.

"Abby," he whispered, yanking his phone out of his pocket. She hadn't called yet. *Can't call this morning,* he typed out quickly as he took a couple of steps toward the chapel. *I'm so sorry. Raincheck?*

No problem, Dad, she messaged back. *I got caught up with Michael.*

Zach's steps stilled. *Michael?* He typed out the question and sent it, his thoughts somewhere else now.

I'll tell you about him when I call, she messaged. *No spoilers, Dad!*

Oh, but he wanted the spoilers. Was Abby seeing someone? She was a beautiful girl, but she had not dated much growing up. She could read lips, but she had a hard time communicating with the boys she went out with.

Michael's probably deaf too, he told himself as he put his phone away. Celia. He was going to enjoy a sermon with Celia. He could get all the juicy details about Abby and this Michael later.

He paused in the doorway, finally finding her when she turned to look behind her. He raised his hand and hurried down the aisle to sit beside her. The pastor was already talking, but Celia had saved him a spot. He barely fit in it, and he lifted his arm to rest it around her shoulders.

She leaned right into him, and Zach swore he heard the gossip mill start right up, the whirring of the engine sounding an awful lot like whispering.

He didn't care. He didn't live here, and Celia was a grown woman. He was a grown man.

In that moment, his heartbeat skipped, stalled, stopped. Owen.

Was this the church Owen went to?

He didn't want to look around and find out. As he listened to the pastor talk about treating everyone with respect, he decided he didn't care. Owen didn't get to decide who Zach spent his time with. Period. The end.

An hour later, he stood with everyone else for the closing hymn, his spirit completely rejuvenated.

And then the people descended.

He shook hands and smiled, tried to hold onto names and faces, but they became a blur. At least until Finn said, "Hello, Zach," with a smile. He knew Finn and Amanda, and he seized onto their momentum taking them toward the lobby.

"Excellent sermon," he told the pastor, and then he and Celia finally escaped the building.

"Wow," he said, taking in a deep breath of the spring air.

"And those weren't even the Whittakers," she said, nodding to something in front of her. "They're over there."

A group of people stood several yards down the sidewalk, chatting with one another. Zach watched them, trying to get a sense of who they were from a distance. Of course, he'd been to the wedding, and everyone had been kind and happy. But these people were important to Celia, and he wanted them to like him too—as more than a wedding guest at an isolated event.

"Do you want to meet them now?" she asked. "Or wait until we get to the lodge?"

"Whatever," he said, taking her hand in his and walking. They arrived at the group, which parted like he was Moses and they were the Red Sea.

"Everyone," Celia said. "This is my boyfriend, Zach. You might remember him from Amanda's wedding." She swallowed, and looked up at Zach, a healthy amount of anxiety in her gaze.

"Zach, these are the Whittaker boys. Graham's the oldest. Then Eli. He's the one who just adopted the baby."

"Of course," Zach said, shaking both of their hands and smiling for all he was worth.

"Then Andrew. He runs Springside."

"Graham runs Springside," Andrew said with a smile, also shaking Zach's hand.

"And Beau," Celia said. "He married Lily, who's one of the Everett Sisters. So Vi and Rose come up to the lodge every week too." She kept going with wives names, and Zach said hello and nodded and shook and smiled.

"All right," the Everett mother said. "Who's driving today? I have a huge pan of oatmeal bars in my car I need to take."

The crowd started to disperse, and Zach stood still and watched them go. "They're great," he said.

"Aren't they?" Celia said, still at his side. "I do love them like family."

"Speaking of which, where's Reagan and Ruth today?" Both of her daughters had moved home after the end of the semester, and they had taken some of Celia's time too. Zach wasn't complaining, but he had noticed a difference in their relationship when he didn't have all of Celia's attention.

"Reagan and Dale went to look at something for the wedding," Celia said. "And Ruth went to Cheyenne for the weekend to see Brandon."

"Sounds fun," Zach said, squeezing her hand. "Should we get up to the lodge? Do you want me to drive?"

"Yes," she said, snuggling into his side. Zach felt powerful and strong with her at his side, and he guided her over to his truck, those three little words teeming against the back of his tongue.

He wasn't going to say them, though. Oh, no, he was not.

He wasn't.

CHAPTER 17

Celia sat right next to Zach in the truck, her own nerves getting the best of her. He seemed tight and on-edge too, and it was no wonder. She'd introduced him to at least three dozen people in the span of ten minutes, and everyone was watching him.

Making judgments about him. About her being with him. Her brothers had been in the congregation, and they'd both texted. She'd ignored their messages, instead finally asking Zach, "What do you—Do you think Owen was there?"

"I don't know," Zach said. "We used to go to this church over by the elementary school growing up." He glanced at her. "He doesn't get to decide, Celia."

She nodded, her lips pressed together into a tense line. Zach had been clear about making his own decisions, but that didn't erase the fact that he'd basically be cutting himself off from his family if he chose to be with her.

They'd spent more time apart in these last few weeks as she worked on Reagan's wedding. The dress was set to be finished later that week, and the flowers had been ordered. Celia had practiced once on the wedding cake, and it had turned out beautiful. Reagan had changed a few things, but Celia felt certain she could get it right on the actual day.

The bridesmaids dresses had been ordered. The venue booked. Reagan and Dale had just gotten pictures taken for their announcements, and she and Reagan would get those addressed and in the mail tomorrow or Tuesday.

Ruth had been a big help as well, keeping up with chores around the house, taking Grizz out for walks, and sampling menu items. Celia loved having her daughters home with her, even if it was only for a month or two.

At the same time, she'd been trying to figure out how to juggle her relationship with Zach with her workload and her family. She thought she'd been doing a decent job of making sure everyone got the attention they needed.

But every once in a while, her familiar doubts would creep up on her, and she couldn't help worrying about Owen, Gene, and Xander, and what they really thought of their brother dating an Abbott.

Before she knew it, Zach pulled into the parking lot at the lodge, and they walked inside together. The atmosphere inside was lively, as usual, and Stockton went roaring by with little Ronnie toddling after him, yelling, "Stocky! Stocky!"

Celia swept the little boy into her arms and planted a kiss on his cheek. "What did he take from you, Ronnie?"

"Nothing," Stockton yelled down the steps. "Me and Bailey are playing up here. Will you tell my dad?" And he was at the top of the steps and down the hall before Celia could answer.

She giggled as the toddler squirmed out of her arms and started to climb the steps too. It would take Ronnie much longer to get up them, and he'd likely find the door closed to the room where Stockton and Bailey were playing.

Graham came into the living room, clearly looking for Ronnie. "He thinks he's going to play with Stockton and Bailey," Celia said, entering the house fully with Zach behind her.

"Come play with Chrissy," Graham said to his son. "Hey, Celia." He gave her a smile and swept a kiss across her forehead as if she were his mother. Sometimes she felt like she was, though she could never replace Amanda.

"Good to have you here, Zach," Graham added, looking back and forth between the two of them, obviously making some sort of connection. "You were Finn's best man."

"That's right," Zach said, smiling. He was a pure gentleman, and in that white shirt and tie and charcoal dress hat, he was cowboy perfection. Warmth moved through Celia as she walked through the living room and into the kitchen, where a couple of the Everett sisters stood in the kitchen.

Rose had an apple in her hand, and Celia grinned at her. "Starving?"

"These babies eat so much," she said, lifting the apple to her lips. "Three more weeks."

"If you last that long," Vi said, eyeing Rose's very pregnant belly. "You look like you're going to pop."

"Rose is carrying triplets," Celia said to Zach, who stood on the fringes of the kitchen, staring at the blonde women.

"And Vi just had twins," he said. "Right? Flower names. Daisy, I think. Mary."

Vi faced him, her face shining with surprise and happiness. "That's right." She looked at Celia, who buried herself in getting out the hamburger buns so she wouldn't have to meet Vi's inquisitive expression. "He's a keeper, Celia."

"You think so?" She laughed as she opened a bag and plucked a knife from the drawer to slice the buns. "You've known him for five minutes."

"And he remembered the names of my children, which means he actually listens to you." At that moment, Todd entered the kitchen carrying both babies.

"They need you," he said, passing one to Vi and keeping the other for himself.

"Excuse me," she said, smiling around at everyone before following her husband out of the kitchen.

Rose finished her apple and threw the core in the garbage can. "Zach, I need your help."

"What can I do?" he asked, stepping forward.

"There's a big swing in the backyard. I need you to get me there safely." She beamed up at him, slipped her hand through his arm, and led him toward the back door. Celia watched them go, a smile stuck on her face.

She'd already been to the lodge today, and she pulled out the cubed watermelon, the potato salad, and the lettuce salad she'd prepared. She sliced tomatoes and tore lettuce leaves while onions caramelized on the stovetop.

Beau came into the kitchen, and she said, "Beau, will you go start the grill, and we'll get the meat on?"

"Sure thing," he said, opening a couple of drawers before he found the lighter stick. "Want me to take out the meat?"

"Yes, please. And send Eli and Andrew or someone to start bringing out everything else."

"On it."

A minute later, Zach entered the kitchen. "Beau said you needed help."

"Everything goes out," she said as more people arrived to help. "Amanda, get all the serving utensils we need."

Celia felt very in control of herself as she worked in the kitchen, and soon enough, everything and everyone was outside. Beau and Lily had commissioned someone to build a picnic table long enough to hold them all, with three umbrellas above to shade everyone.

The food had been set on another table, this one almost as long as the picnic table, and Beau stood at the grill with Graham as they talked about something.

Celia paused and took in the scene, joy and peace

filling her from top to bottom. Tears pricked her eyes, and she couldn't imagine being anywhere else, with anyone else. Especially when her eyes landed on Zach and how easily he conversed with Fran and Jack Everett, who stood with Finn and Amanda.

"Ready," Beau said, and everyone gathered over near the food table for a prayer. With that done, the chaos erupted as parents helped their kids get food. Celia usually went last through the line, but today, she stepped in front of Zach and started filling her plate.

They sat right in the middle of the picnic table, others filling in around them as they brought their food over. Zach touched her arm, and she turned to look at him. Everything else fell away.

"You're incredible," he whispered, those dark eyes somehow so bright.

She leaned her forehead against his, and said, "I think I'm falling for you."

He'd used those words a few weeks ago when they'd been in Cheyenne for Reagan's graduation. She hadn't repeated them then. But she certainly felt like she was falling, and it wouldn't be long before she was all the way in love with him.

He'd own her heart then, and she couldn't imagine what she'd do if he squeezed it too hard. Or if Owen came and trampled on it.

Putting her doubts and fears out of her mind, she turned back to her food, back to the conversations around her, back to this place where she'd always belonged.

THE AFTERNOON SLIPPED AWAY with good conversation and the sound of children's laughter. Several people went horseback riding, but Celia stayed on the back patio with Zach, Eli's new baby in her arms.

She was aware Zach had watched her quite a few times, and she'd offered Isaiah to him a couple of times. He hadn't taken the baby from her yet, but she really wanted him to.

Rose and Liam had stayed in the swing on the patio for almost the whole afternoon, and she yelped as she put both hands on her pregnant belly.

Celia's heartbeat raced as adrenaline poured through her. As Liam asked, "Baby, are you all right?"

A groan came out of Rose's mouth that didn't sound entirely human. "Something's...wrong...." She panted and tried to stand but couldn't.

"I'm calling an ambulance," Beau said.

"My water broke," Rose said, her voice full of pain. She turned to look at Liam, pure panic on her face. "I can't have the babies here, Liam." In the next moment, her face crumpled with pain again, and Liam put his hand on her back.

"Baby," he said calmly. "I think you're going to have to be flexible." He looked at Beau, who was still on the phone. "Tell them bring incubators and heat lamps. Three babies."

"I'm going to call her doctor," Lily said.

Celia stood up and handed baby Isaiah to Zach, whether he wanted him or not. "Liam, what should I do? Where do you need her?"

"Let's see if we can get her inside," Liam said, still so calm. "One of the bedrooms down by Lily's."

"I'm not having the babies here," Rose said, standing as both Celia and Liam helped her on either side. She looked fierce and determined, but absolutely terrified. Celia understood the feeling. She'd been in situations she couldn't control and couldn't even think about.

When she'd lost Brandon...her denial had been strong for quite a while. Almost like she believed he would return to her by some miracle.

"It's okay, love," Liam said. "Let's just get inside anyway, okay?"

Rose took a tentative step, her breathing labored, and both hands still holding her belly as if she could keep the babies inside that way.

"Celia, as soon as we get her settled, could you start heating some towels?" Liam asked.

"Liam," Rose said, tears splashing down her face. "We can't have the babies here. What if—?"

"Sh," he said, cutting her off though he wore a bit of anxiety in his expression now. "Lily's getting Doctor Simmons. Beau's called the paramedics. I'm a doctor, baby. Everything will be fine."

Celia cast a glance at Zach, who had also stood, that baby cradled perfectly in his arms. She couldn't help the strong attraction to him in that moment, though she was in the midst of another crisis.

She couldn't walk side-by-side with Rose and Liam once they reached the hall, but she followed, her hand still on Rose's elbow. Every step seemed to take a lifetime, but Liam finally got her situated in the bedroom in the corner. She cried openly now, panting through a contraction while Liam stripped the bed and Celia ran to grab towels.

He laid them over the mattress and helped his wife climb into bed. Another contraction came, and Celia wasn't timing, but it seemed like only a couple of minutes had passed since the last one.

"I'll go get the towels heating," she said, hurrying out of the room again. She brought the door almost all the way closed as Lily rounded the corner.

"He'll be here in thirty minutes."

"I don't know if she has that long," Celia said. "She's contracting every few minutes."

Pure fear crossed Lily's face as she'd had a premature baby—in the hospital. Beau joined them in the hall. "Twenty minutes. They're bringing incubators and heat lamps and everything for a delivery."

"Maybe we should get her in the car and go down," Celia said. "Meet them, even."

"No," Lily said, shaking her head. "Rose won't want to have her babies on the side of the road. She's already upset she might have to have them here."

Beau put his arm around her. "It'll be okay."

But Lily didn't say anything. She moved over to the

door and pushed it open gently. "Rose, honey? The ambulance is going to be here real soon."

"We need water," Liam said from within the room. "Maybe I should've put her in the tub."

"I am not having my babies in a tub," Rose practically screeched, and Celia smiled.

"I'll get the water and the towels warming," she said. "Come get me if there's anything else you need."

Beau nodded and let her go, frozen to the spot close to the door but not close enough to see in.

Celia pulled as many towels from the linen closet as she could find and went into the kitchen. The dryer probably wouldn't be hot enough to warm them properly, so she pulled baking sheets from the cupboards in the kitchen and stacked them into piles before sliding them into the oven.

She adjusted the heat on that and turned to find Zach standing there holding that baby. "Hey, how is she?"

"She's going to have those babies in about fifteen minutes," Celia said, worry needling through her.

Zach looked down at the baby in his arms. "He's so perfect."

Celia stepped over to him. "He is, isn't he?" She gazed at the baby too, and then up at Zach. Careful not to smash Isaiah, she tipped up onto her toes and kissed Zach. "Can you hold him while I deal with the towels?" she whispered against his lips.

"Of course," he said, touching his forehead to hers. "Yell at me if you need something." And with that, he took Isaiah into the living room to the rocking recliner where she'd held him weeks ago.

"Celia," Beau called from down the hall, and she turned that way, hoping one of the babies hadn't come quite yet.

CHAPTER 18

Zach rocked with the baby, glad he could help in some small way as many others scurried around the lodge, trying to help Rose Murphy. He'd delivered animals on the farm before, but he couldn't imagine having three babies at home.

Rose didn't seem too happy about it either, but Zach knew some things couldn't be helped.

"Thank you so much," Meg said, pausing with a stack of towels in her hand. "He's okay?"

"He's fine." Zach grinned up at her. "If there's something else I should be doing, let me know."

"You're helping a ton," she said. "I've sent Eli to get the car seats. The paramedics should be here soon." She glanced toward the front door like she might be able to see through it and determine where the ambulance was.

"No babies yet?"

"Not yet," she said. "I should go. Liam needs help, and

I have some nursing training." She smiled at him and hurried away.

Zach listened to the chaos, content to just watch it. Only a minute later, two heavy fists knocked on the front door and said, "Paramedics."

"Oh, thank goodness," Celia said, rushing past him and toward the door. She pulled it open and added, "Come in. Through the living room, down the hall to the left. Go."

"She's in labor?" the man asked.

"Yes," Celia said, standing back out of the way. "Pregnant with triplets."

The man and woman entered, laden with medical equipment and bags. A third paramedic entered, carrying infant incubators and more equipment. "Ma'am," he said. "How far along is she?"

"Her husband's a doctor," Celia said, following them. "He says she's almost fully dilated, but she hasn't started pushing yet."

"Good," he said. "Sounds like we won't be transporting, Bobby."

"Nope," the man up front said, turning to go down the hall. They moved with absolute confidence, no panic or tension in them at all.

"Her husband's a doctor?" the woman asked.

"Yes," Celia said from behind. "He runs the clinic at the hospital. He's not an OBGYN. That doctor should be here soon, though." Her voice faded as she rounded the corner with them, and Zach marveled at all she could do.

Rose's regular obstetrician arrived a few minutes later, and Zach had only hummed his way through two nursery rhymes before he heard a brand-new baby crying from down the hall.

His chest squeezed, and he smiled a wobbly grin down at Isaiah. "A cousin was just born," he whispered to the baby, the thought of a new life in this world wonderful and beautiful.

Babies were such a blessing, and he once again couldn't wait to become a grandfather. Holding this baby brought him absolute joy.

Several seconds later, Lily joined him in the living room, the newborn swaddled in a pale blue blanket. Tears streamed down her face, but she gave him a happy smile nonetheless.

"Everything okay?" he asked.

"Other than Rose having the babies at home, yes." She sat on the couch. "And not even her home. But it's okay. Everything is okay." She gazed down at the baby. "This one is a boy. Rose and Liam didn't find out if they were having boys or girls."

"Has she named him?"

"Not yet." Lily stroked the baby's head. "But he has so much hair."

Peace existed in the room, and several minutes later, Vi entered the room too. "Another boy." The baby in her arms fussed, and she adjusted the yellow blanket with teddy bears on it to be tighter around him.

"Where are your babies?" Lily asked.

"Todd got them to sleep upstairs," Vi whispered.

The third baby didn't come out, and Zach assumed Rose had kept it with her. Celia entered the living room, her eyes wet. "The last baby is a girl," she said. "Rose and Liam are naming them now, and they would like all the babies back in the bedroom."

Vi and Lily stood and went down the hall. Celia met Zach's eyes, and she looked absolutely radiant though she was crying.

"Come take this one," he said, scooting to the edge of the recliner. She did, and he stood. "I have to get back to my farm." He placed a kiss on her forehead. "You can get a ride back home?"

"Of course." She tipped her head back and kissed him, the sweetest union he'd ever experienced. "Three babies, Zach. Born right here."

"Crazy," he murmured against her lips. "Call me later, okay?"

She nodded and turned toward Rose's mother when she said, "Celia? Rose would like to see you."

Zach watched her bustle away again, absolute love for her filling his heart.

DREAD REPLACED that love the moment his farmhouse came into view. Owen's truck sat in the driveway, its owner sitting on the tailgate, whittling. He'd clearly been there for a while, if the pile of shavings on the ground testified of anything.

"Hey," Zach said easily as he pulled up. "What's going on?" His brother rarely came to Saltgrass Farm—usually only if Zach called him to come help with something extreme.

"Are Mom and Dad okay?" he asked with Owen still hadn't so much as acknowledged that Zach had arrived.

Owen finally lifted his head and looked at Zach. "I told Dad about you and Celia."

Zach pressed his teeth together and looked out the windshield. He wanted to go back in time and rip this feud out of their history. He wanted to challenge his brother and his lifelong hatred. How was that Christlike? Shouldn't he have forgiven the Abbotts by now?

"Did you know that Lennox Abbott has been bringing you gifts for years?" he asked instead, unsure of why that question had come out.

"Lee deals with him," Owen said darkly.

"Why can't you let it go?" Zach asked. "It's been almost one hundred years. You have water rights now. Let it *go*."

"They wronged our family," Owen said. "And she will *never* be welcome with us."

Zach nodded, his anger rising with every second Owen stayed. "I have to go," he said. "I have chores and then Abby's calling."

"I'll help with the chores."

"I don't need your help," Zach said, pushing the button to open his garage so he could pull in.

Owen didn't care what Zach said, because he joined him in the garage and then the house. Zach greeted his dogs, but they couldn't truly comfort him, especially with Owen's presence in the house.

"Really, Owen. Just go."

Owen simply opened the back door and went outside to the farm. Zach sighed, unsure of what to do. Owen really was the most stubborn man on the planet, and if he wanted to help with the chores, he would.

Zach didn't speak to him, and his brother didn't need instructions for how to feed chickens or water goats. The chores got done quickly, and Zach headed for the house, hoping his brother would leave now.

"Gene and Xander think I'm right," Owen said as he washed his hands. "And Dad was livid."

"This is why I live in Dog Valley," Zach said. "You've already driven me away. The family, this feud, all the hatred. I don't get it."

"I told you to end things with her."

"I'm in love with her," Zach said, realizing the words were a huge mistake the moment he said them.

Owen started laughing, the sound crazed and power-ful. Zach would never get the sound out of his ears, and he stalked away from his brother. The feelings of peace and love up at the lodge felt a lifetime away, and he craved that sense of family and belonging more than he ever had.

He hadn't even known a family like that could exist.

His had always been so dysfunctional and removing himself from it hadn't done what he'd hoped it would. Sure, maybe he'd enjoyed a few decades of semi-peace, only going to visit the family farm on holidays or other special occasions.

He'd worked hard after the divorce to be involved in his children's lives, and he had good relationships with them. Lindsey, Abby, and Paul didn't know about the feud, but all of Owen's children did. All of Gene's. All of Xander's. It would never be over.

Zach would forever be the black sheep, and if he kept Celia in his life, she would never be welcome, just as Owen had said.

"You can't run from the past," Owen called after him.

Zach spun back. "Of course you can't," he said. "But you don't have to keep living in it either."

"They stole from us!" Owen yelled.

Zach marched toward him, his fists curling. He hated these feelings of contention, but he'd asked Owen to leave more than once. "They bought the land where the water rights were. *Bought* it."

"They could've shared with us." Owen's chest heaved. His eyes flashed dark fire. His fingers balled into fists too. Zach had been slugged by his brother in the past, and he was too old to take it now.

He stopped several feet away. "But they didn't, Owen. That was their choice, a long time ago. And we've let it poison us for generations. Too long." He shook his head. "For far too long."

"We've always been two steps behind them since," Owen said.

"So what?" Zach challenged. "Have you not had enough to eat? Did your kids go without? Heck, did we ever go without? Because I don't remember that if we did."

His brother's jaw clenched, and Zach shook his head. "Let it go."

"I can't."

Zach didn't know how to help Owen. It seemed impossible that they'd been raised by the same parents. "Then just go," he said. "Leave me alone. I'll leave you alone."

"You'd do that? Cut us all out of your life?"

"I didn't cut you out," Zach said, his frustration rising again. "*You've* done that to me." He fell back a step, and then another. "Abby's calling in ten minutes. Please. Just leave."

Owen nodded once, then twice. "Fine. But Dad wants you to come see him."

"Fine," Zach said, though he would not be doing that. At this point, he'd say anything to get Owen to leave.

"He said he'd drive up here if you didn't, and you know he can't be doing that."

"Then tell him not to bother," Zach said.

"You'd be responsible for him trying to come see you? He could break another hip."

"He's eighty-six-years-old," Zach said. "He makes his own choices."

"I'll tell him you're coming."

"You do that."

Owen stared at him for several long seconds, and he still looked like he'd rip Zach limb from limb. Then he turned and stomped out the door that led to the garage.

Relief washed through Zach, but he didn't experience any happiness. Only grief that his brother and his father were so hard-hearted.

He opened his laptop, and Abby called only thirty seconds later. "Dad," she said in her unique voice, the strange tonalities of it echoing through the kitchen.

"Abby." He jumped over in front of the laptop, the kitchen sink still running. "I was just getting a drink." He did the sign language, and added, "Be right back." He filled a glass with water, turned off the sink, and sat down in front of the laptop. "Okay, I'm here. Tell me about Michael."

She smiled and laughed, her signs flashing like lightning. She'd gotten so much faster since going to school in D.C., and Zach didn't communicate with her regularly enough to be able to read that fast.

"Slow down," he said with a chuckle. "And yes, I went right for the jugular. You can't just mention a man and expect me not to have questions."

Abby made an exaggerated show of rolling her eyes, but she did slow down her signs. He was able to keep up as she told him about a guy she'd met at work. He'd ordered a pork enchilada and gotten a taco, and Abby had been *so impressed* with how nice he was about it, that she'd "maybe started flirting with him."

His friends all left, but he'd stayed during the rest of her shift, and they'd talked, and walked, and he'd asked her out.

"Did you kiss him that night?"

"Dad," she said, her voice coming over the speakers again.

"You did," Zach said, surprise moving through him. Lindsey had always been the flirtatious one, with plenty of dates. His father-heart had always hurt for Abby, but she seemed so happy now. So, so happy.

He's a nice guy, Abby signed. *We've been seeing each other for a couple of months now.*

"And you're just telling me?" Zach continued to sign without talking. *You seem so happy, talking about him.*

I am happy, Dad.

Did he have anything to do with your decision to stay in D.C. this summer? She'd always come home for summer break, and he'd always gotten to see her for half of that.

Maybe, Abby said with a smile.

"Right," Zach said with a laugh. "Maybe. I see how it is."

What about you and Celia? Abby signed. *You've been ten times happier than usual.*

"Ten times?" Zach rolled his eyes now. "I'm sure that's not true."

Abby paused, her eyes somehow seeing things other humans couldn't. It was like the Lord had made her extra-observant to make up for her lack of hearing. "Dad," she said. "What happened?" She signed as she spoke, and Zach loved the sound of her voice, flawed as it was.

"Nothing happened," he said, signing even slower now. He didn't want Abby to know about the feud, or his fight with his brother, or that he'd fallen in love with Celia. "I met everyone she works with up at the lodge today," he said instead, continuing to tell her about Rose's babies and how everyone there had come together in a moment of need.

Abby let the topic of Celia go, but Zach knew she'd text him all week. They signed off, and Zach leaned away from the laptop, utterly spent.

And when his phone rang, and Celia's name lit up the screen, he didn't have the heart to answer it.

CHAPTER 19

C elia spent the new few days at the lodge or Rose's house, stocking up the fridge and freezers in both places with plenty of food. She loved holding the tiny babies in the hospital, where everyone had been transported once the triplets were born.

Rose had named them Collin, Jackson, and Clover, and Celia smiled every time she thought about them.

Reagan's wedding was only two weeks away now, and Celia needed to dig in and get everything done. She couldn't get Zach to pick up the phone, so she just texted him that she couldn't come up to Saltgrass for a couple of weeks, and he'd said, *That's fine.*

Celia scrolled through her texts to his name and tapped on it. He hadn't initiated any conversations since the day at the lodge, and something writhed in her blood. When she'd gotten busy with the wedding before, he'd brought her food. Texted her all evening. Told her how much he missed her.

This silence felt strange, and she dialed him again. He didn't answer. Again. She hadn't left any messages before, but she did now. "Hey," she said, unsure of what else to say. "I'm just...I haven't heard your voice in a while, and I miss you. Will you call me please?"

She hung up and turned back to the boxes that had come that day. Reagan should be coming out to help unpack the things they'd ordered online, but Celia didn't want to wait. She sliced through the tape and looked inside at all the bags of butter mints.

Reagan had chosen navy blue, eggplant, and silver as her colors, and she'd found a website where she could order candy in any colors she wanted.

"You started already?" Reagan asked, coming up beside Celia. "Hey, Mom."

"How's Dale?" she asked.

"Good. The tuxedo fit, and he's got it now. So that's good news."

"And we've got the final dress fitting tomorrow," Celia said. "I'm doing all the grocery shopping for the cake this week too, just to make sure I can get everything I need."

"Where's your checklist?" Reagan teased as she pulled out a bag of silver-tinted mints. "Have the mirrors come yet?"

"I haven't seen them," Celia said. They'd rented a venue, but all that included was the space, the sound system, and the tables and chairs. All the décor was up to them, and she and Reagan had put together something Celia hoped would be elegant but not cost her an arm and a leg.

"We have the candles. The confetti. The mints and chocolates." Reagan ticked the items off on her fingers. "The Roundhouse Gardens are providing the refreshments."

"Besides the cake."

"Right." Reagan looked at her mother, and their gazes held. "Mom." She drew in a deep breath. "Thank you for all you've done. All you're doing."

Emotion welled up inside Celia, sticking somewhere in the back of her throat. "Of course," she said. "I hope you only get married once." She didn't want to project any of her fears onto Reagan, so she left it at that. "And it should be special, even if you don't care about the details."

"Who doesn't care about details?" Ruth asked, entering the house through the back door, Grizz behind her. The dog went right over to his water bowl and started lapping while Ruth joined them at the table.

"Ooh, butter mints." She reached for a package and hesitated. "Can I open this and have one?"

"I don't know," Reagan said. "You're the one who knew how many bags to order."

Ruth grinned at her sister. "Then we have enough for me to eat a few right now." She tore into the bag and popped one of the dark blue mints into her mouth. "Mm." She bent to unclip the leash from Grizz's collar. "Oh, Mom, I ran into someone on our walk this morning."

"Oh?" Celia knew a lot of people in Coral Canyon, as she'd lived here for her entire life.

"Yeah," Ruth said. "And he wasn't very nice. Told me to tell you to end things with your boyfriend."

"I asked him who he was, but he just drove off."

"What was he driving?"

"A truck. Black truck."

A cowboy then. Definitely a Zuckerman.

She shrugged, hoping she did a good job playing it off as nothing. But Reagan had stilled, and she looked at Celia. "Who would tell you to break up with Zach?"

Celia sighed and pulled out a chair. She sank into it and stared at the tabletop. "Girls, my family...a long time ago, my family did something to the Zuckermans that they haven't been able to let go of. There's sort of a feud between Abbotts and Zuckermans."

"A feud? Those still exist?" Ruth poured a cup of coffee and set it in front of her mother.

"Apparently." Celia said. "And I can't get Zach to pick up the phone when I call him."

"That's not good," Reagan said, abandoning the unpacking and sitting at the table too. "How long has it been since you've spoken to him? Actually spoken to him?"

"A few days."

"When?" Reagan asked.

Celia met her eye. "Sunday."

"Five days," she looked at Ruth. "Crisis mode."

"Crisis mode?" Celia asked, looking back and forth between her daughters. "What does that mean?"

"How did you leave things with Zach on Sunday?" Ruth asked.

"Fine," she said. "Rose had the triplets, and he had to leave to go do his farm chores."

"And did you call him that night?"

"Yes," she said slowly. "And he didn't answer. But he was talking with his daughter, and maybe he was busy." Celia wanted him to be busy. Be on the call with Abby. Simply be too tired to talk. Something.

"He's not avoiding me," Celia said. "Is he?"

"How many times have you called?" Reagan asked.

"I hate all these questions," Celia said. "You two are like detectives." She lifted her coffee mug to her lips, her nerves already feeling jittery.

"How many times, Mom?"

"Every day," she muttered to her hot drink. "But that's normal for us. We talk every day."

"Okay," Ruth said, pulling in a breath. "So let's recap. See? That wasn't a question." She grinned at Celia, but her dark eyes remained serious. "You've been dating this guy for three months. You're at a talk-everyday-on-the-phone level, and you've called five times now, where he hasn't answered." She punctuated her statement with raised eyebrows.

Celia hated how that sounded. "He's avoiding me."

Reagan nodded. "But the real question is why. What happened on Sunday night that you don't know about?"

"Who was in the black truck?" Ruth mused.

Celia knew who was in the black truck. "His brother, I'm assuming," she said. "He has three of them, and they all still have very strong feelings about the feud."

"What about Uncle Mack and Uncle Lennox?" Ruth asked. "Maybe they can do something."

"They've tried." Celia ran her hands through her hair, a strong feeling of desperation pulling through her. "I knew this would be a problem from the beginning. I was stupid enough to believe it wouldn't be."

"Mom." Reagan put her hand over Celia's. "You're not stupid."

"What has Zach said about his family?" Ruth asked.

"He said they don't get to decide." Celia stood up, took keyed up to sit still for another second. "But they obviously do. It's fine. I'm fine." She brushed her hair out of her face. "I left him a message today. Let's finish getting this stuff unpacked so we can move down the list."

Ruth and Reagan didn't argue, but they didn't jump up and start unboxing either. Celia didn't look at them, and the silence in the kitchen was almost as bad as what she was experiencing with Zach.

"I wish your dad could be here for the wedding," she whispered, sudden tears coming to her eyes.

"Mom." Reagan wrapped her arms around Celia, and she had to give up trying to take mints out of the box. Ruth hugged them both, and Celia let herself cry.

For Brandon.

For Zach.

And for herself.

AFTER THE DRESS FITTING. The grocery shopping. The cooking. The cleaning. The final checklisting, Celia dressed in a pair of slacks that made her feel comfortable and a purple blouse that made her feel sexy.

Then she drove to Dog Valley.

Zach had not called her back. He had not texted her. It had been nine days since the last time she'd seen him or really spoken to him, and she could not go another day with this silence.

Reagan was getting married on Sunday and then moving hundreds of miles away, and she wanted Zach at her side at the wedding. If she had to go through it alone…she couldn't even imagine that.

She hadn't had to imagine it, because she had Zach. Her strong, steady Zach. What had happened on Sunday?

Normally, she'd text him as she turned, and he'd open the garage door for her so she could pull in. He'd meet her at the trunk and take the bulk of the groceries into the house.

Today, she pulled into his driveway, noting that his yard looked freshly mowed. The bushes trimmed and everything exactly right. The man had an eye for detail, and she sure did like coming to this farmhouse.

She'd stood on these steps before and rung the doorbell. Her anxiety shot into the sky as she stood there and waited. He didn't come to the door, and she knocked and rang the doorbell again.

When he still didn't come, but she heard a dog barking somewhere behind the house, she went around the side and through the gate into the backyard. The farm spread before her, and one of Zach's golden retrievers came jogging toward her.

"Hey, girl." She scratched along the dog's head and scanned the landscape behind her. "Where's Zach, huh?" She wasn't sure how he would react to her showing up. He was a smart guy. He hadn't forgotten to call her, and he knew he'd cut her out of his life.

What she wanted to know was why.

The dog trotted off and turned back, looking at Celia like, *Well? Come on. I'll take you to him.*

She followed the dog, noting how everything on the farm seemed to be inside a chalk outline. A few goats grazed in a small field, and the henhouse looked freshly painted.

The dog went into a big barn at the end of the lane, and Celia hesitated just outside the door. "Zach?" she called, and something hit the floor inside the barn.

A few moments and several footsteps later, and Zach appeared in the doorway, a dirty towel in his hands. "Celia."

So many things rushed through her. Rage. Fear. Hope. Love. "What's going on?" she asked. "You haven't taken any of my calls in a long time." Her voice stayed steady, but it sounded whiny to her ears. She didn't want to be whiny.

He ducked his head, and Celia looked at the towel. Blood seeped through it, and she said, "You cut yourself."

"Yeah."

"Let's go take care of it in the house." She turned and walked away, overly relieved that Zach came with her.

"Listen," he said. "I've just been trying to figure out what to say."

"What happened?"

"Owen was here when I got back last Sunday." Zach spoke quieter than she'd ever heard him speak before. "He told my dad about us. Everyone knows now. No one's happy. I don't know what to do."

Celia nodded, her eyes on the ground. She checked his hand, and it looked bad judging by the way the bloodstain kept getting larger. "So you thought you'd just stop talking to me."

"I don't know." He sounded completely lost, and while Celia was frustrated with him, she still felt bad for him.

"Sit down," she said once they got inside. He complied, and when he took the towel off his hand, he hissed.

"This is bad," he said as the blood started to pool again. "I need stitches."

Celia looked at the gash in his palm. "What were you doing out there?"

"Cutting leather."

"You need to go to the hospital," she agreed. "Let's go. I'll drive."

"Celia," he said, looking fully into her eyes. She saw the anguish, the regret, the pain. "Things are so complicated."

"You said they didn't get to decide," she said, wishing the way he'd removed her from his life didn't hurt so much.

"I know." He closed his eyes, swaying, and Celia realized in that moment that he was going to faint.

"Whoa. Zach." She grabbed onto his shoulders, but he easily weighed twice as much as her, and there was no way she could hold him upright on a barstool. She did the best she could to make sure his head didn't hit the floor too hard, and then she called 911.

CHAPTER 20

Zach woke up in a moving vehicle. Machines beeped around him, and voices talked, and he couldn't remember getting there. A groan came out of his mouth.

"Hey," someone said. A face appeared above him. "You're okay. You're in an ambulance, on the way to the Dog Valley Hospital. We'll be there in two minutes. I'm Jerome."

"Jerome," Zach said, everything rushing back into his brain. How he hadn't eaten breakfast that morning. The slice of the hatchet across his palm. The walk back to the farmhouse with Celia. "Where's Celia?"

"She's following us in her car," Jerome said. "You're okay. We've got the bleeding contained, but you're going to need stitches."

"And a CAT scan," another voice said. "You hit your head when you fell, and Celia said your head didn't hit too hard, but we all want to make sure you haven't hurt your neck or back."

Zach wanted to nod, but his head was strapped down tight. He couldn't move it left or right, forward or back, up or down. He let his eyes close, the movement of the ceiling above him making him nauseous.

His behavior over the past nine days made him sick too. Maybe that was why he hadn't eaten breakfast. Couldn't even stomach a swallow of coffee.

Everything in him felt stitched too tight. He hadn't known what to say to Celia, so he'd gone silent. Immature, for sure, and he was eternally glad she hadn't let him simply disappear out of her life. Of course, now he'd have to have a hard conversation with her in public, while he had pain and thread in his hand.

He couldn't think about that now. He let the movement of the ambulance beneath him comfort him. Everything was going to be okay. His hand would get fixed, and he'd heal.

Zach could only hope the same was true for his heart.

BY THE TIME the doctors and nurses left him alone in a semi-private room, he hadn't seen Celia for a couple of hours. Fourteen stitches now lived in his palm, and they pulled uncomfortably.

He'd been dehydrated, so they'd hooked him up to an

IV, and now he just needed someone to bring him something to eat.

Zach thought about who'd he call in this situation. Before the wedding a few months ago, he'd have called Owen.

Now, the only person he wanted to see was Celia.

As if summoned by his thoughts, a light knock sounded on the door, and she poked her head into the room. "Are you up for a visitor?"

He tried to sit up straighter, because lying in this hospital bed was stupid. He felt weak. He hadn't hurt his legs, his back, or his head. She'd saved him from a worse injury, and gratitude for her filled him.

"Of course."

A quick smile touched her mouth for a moment, and she slipped into the room, a white deli bag clutched in one fist. "The doctors said you were complaining about being hungry." She lifted the bag. "I ran out and got you a roast beef sandwich."

She was easily an angel. "Thank you, Celia," he said. He took the bag with his good hand and took out the sandwich. The first bite had his taste buds rejoicing, and the food allowed him to put off the conversation they needed to have.

Celia sat in the only other chair, and she busied herself on her phone. Zach actually hated that she didn't start the conversation, though she had driven up to Dog Valley to confront him.

"How are things going with the wedding?" he asked. "Busy, I assume."

"I've been busy, yes," she said. "But not too busy for a phone call, or to text."

He almost choked on his bite of roast beef, cheese, and bread. Their eyes met, and Zach felt her displeasure all the way down into his soul. "I'm sorry," he said.

"Are you?"

"Of course."

She looked doubtful, and Zach crumpled up the wrapper from his sandwich and put it back in the bag. "I don't know what to do." He'd told her this at the farmhouse before passing out.

"I understand," she said.

"Do you?" he asked. "Because I don't."

"Things are complicated," she said. "Relationships always are, and blending two families always is." She leaned forward, her pretty eyes intense. "And we're not just doing that already, what with our children and pasts and all of that. But we're trying to merge two families that have hated each other for a long time."

"My kids like you," he said.

"And mine like you." She reached out and traced her hand down the side of his face. "But I don't think you're ready."

"Ready for what?"

She stood up and paced away from him as if she'd leave. His heart jumped around, and she could hear it as he was connected to a monitor.

Facing him again, she said, "I can't ask you to give up your family."

"I told you they didn't get to decide."

"But then you let them decide." She looked like she might cry, but no tears trickled down her face. "You cut me off as soon as your dad found out."

"I—" He didn't know how to explain. "I went and saw him last week. He's old, Celia. So set in his ways. Neither of my parents could understand why I'd even talk to you."

"Hatred can run deep," she said. "It's okay. I'll be okay."

"Wait. You'll be...okay? What are you saying?"

"I'm saying I can't ask you to go against your family."

"I'm fifty years old."

"And yet," she said.

He waited for the rest of her sentence, but she didn't deliver it. She gave a small shrug. "I think you've shown me what you're willing to do," she said, her chin wobbling. She swiped at her eyes, and her voice sounded like she'd inhaled helium when she said, "You couldn't even call me back."

Celia took a few steps toward the door, and Zach felt like the best thing in his life was leaving.

"Wait," he said.

She turned back, and he swung his legs over the edge of the bed and got up. "I don't want you to go. Not like this."

Celia gave him a watery smile and met him halfway across the room. She did not step into his arms. Instead, she reached up with one hand and ran her fingers down the side of his face.

"I never lied to you," she said. "When I said you were the best thing in my life, I meant it." Those lovely eyes filled with tears. "Reagan's wedding is on Sunday. You know my number."

And with that, she walked to the door, opened it, and left.

Zach's whole body wailed at her departure, but he couldn't get his voice to call her back. He'd never lied to her either, and she was absolutely the best thing in his life.

But—

He was so tired of buts.

But he'd never been able to go to another family function.

But he couldn't betray his father.

But he didn't know what to say. Didn't know what to do.

They all sounded like weak excuses when faced with the reality of life without Celia.

His phone rang, and he turned toward the counter, where the sound came from. Surprise filled him, as he didn't remember putting his phone there.

Paul's name sat on the screen, and Zach hurried to swipe on the call and lift his phone to his ear. "Hey, bud," he said, and his voice sounded mostly normal.

"Dad," Paul said. "Where are you? There's blood all

over the kitchen, and you're not here. But your truck is in the garage."

"I'm at the hospital, but I'm fine," he said quickly. "I forgot you were coming today. Sorry I didn't call."

"What happened?"

Everything from that morning zipped through his head, exhausting him. "I'm in room 314. I'll tell you when you get here."

Paul said he'd be right there, and Zach took the chair Celia had been sitting in. Paul would drive him home. Paul would keep him company. And maybe Paul could help him figure out what to do about Celia.

❦

"WHAT DO you mean *you think* you broke up?" Paul knelt on the floor, wiping up the dried blood there. His luggage sat by the front door, and his presence in Zach's house was very welcome. He'd be living with Zach for the summer, when he'd then return to school in the fall.

"You either break up or you don't. There's usually not a question mark involved."

"She said her daughter's wedding was on Sunday," Zach said from his spot on the couch. He felt bad making his son clean up, but he couldn't really do it with one hand. He had a feeling he'd need a lot of help around the farm, and another rush of gratitude for his son bled through him.

At the same time, if Paul wasn't here, Zach knew he'd

have asked Owen, or Gene, or Xander to come help. And if he didn't have them to ask? What would he do then?

"She said I knew her phone number," Zach said. "So I don't know if we broke up or not."

"Dad." Paul stood up. "You like this lady, right?"

"Yes," Zach whispered.

"Then call her," Paul said. "It's not that complicated."

"Isn't it?" Zach asked. "I won't be able to take her to anything at my family's farm. Ever."

"So what?" Paul asked. "You barely go down there anyway, and you don't care what they think of you. That's why you and Mom came to Dog Valley, right?"

Zach couldn't argue. He wasn't sure when he'd gotten so far into his head. "I need to go see my dad again." He stood up. "Can you drive me?"

"Now?" Paul asked. "Dad, you've had an eventful day already."

"Yes," Zach said. "Now." The last visit had not gone well, and Zach had not stood up for himself. His father had taught Zach to work hard and be respectful, but Zach had lived most of his life in fear of disappointing his dad.

"All right," Paul said. "But I'm bringing my laptop and not coming in. I have some work to do."

Zach nodded and started for the garage. His children did not have a strong relationship with his parents, as Kathy had moved to Jackson after the divorce. Paul barely knew them, and Zach wasn't going to make him start building a bond now.

He had moved to Dog Valley years ago to get away

from the bitterness that seemed to consume the Zucker-mans, and with every mile Paul drove toward the farm where Zach had grown up, he remembered how much he'd wanted to leave the place.

"They live in the cabin to the left," he said when the buildings on the farm came into view. "Right over there." He pointed, and Paul went down the left fork in the lane. "I'll try to be fast."

"Take your time," Paul said. "I can work from anywhere."

Zach smiled at him, once again grateful his son had chosen to come stay with him. Paul usually did, staying all summer. Zach knew it hadn't been easy for him, as he'd left his friends and sports teams in Jackson to spend time with Zach on a small farm an hour away.

Climbing the steps, Zach whispered a prayer under his breath, begging the Lord for guidance, for the right words, for clarity of mind.

"Dad?" he called as he knocked on the door. He didn't wait for someone to get up and answer. Both of his parents were semi-immobile, and when he didn't see them sitting in the living room, he crossed through the cabin to the back porch.

Sure enough, they both sat there, his mother with a book in her hands and his father just looking out over the land he'd worked for decades.

"Hey," Zach said, also taking a moment to appreciate the farm spread before him. He loved open land, the good smell of the earth, and the way the sun gave life and light to the world.

"Zach," his mother said, letting her book fall to her lap. "What are you doing here?"

"I—"

"What happened to your hand?" She reached for it, barely brushing her fingers against the bandages.

"Oh, I cut myself," he said. "I had to get stitches." He sighed, as if the stitches were the worst part of the last nine days. But they weren't. Not even close.

"Dad. Mom. I'm in love with Celia Armstrong, and I'm not going to stop seeing her."

"We've talked about this, son." His dad's gruff voice sounded tired, not angry.

"Yeah," Zach said. "And I made a mistake. I just wanted you to know that I love you both. But I love her too, and I don't want to lose the best thing in my life because of something I don't believe in anyway."

"You don't believe in family loyalty?" his mother asked.

"I believe in forgiveness," Zach said. "And kindness. And love. And Celia is all of those things." At least he hoped she was, because he needed her forgiveness. "So I love you and Dad, and Owen, Gene, and Xander. I love their wives and their children, but that doesn't mean I have to choose to spend my time with them."

"You've already made that clear, Zach," his dad said.

He nodded, because he supposed he had. "I love you

guys. I don't want to hurt you. But it's time the feud ended."

"They stole—"

"I know, Dad." Zach exhaled, trying not to make it sound like he was frustrated. But he was, and tired, and so done with trying to hate the Abbotts. "I know. And I'm sorry they hurt you. I think they've tried to make up for it over the years. It's *us* who've been unforgiving. Unrepentant. Unyielding. You, and Owen, and...."

He turned back to the door. "It doesn't matter. I'm just letting you know that I love you, and my door will always be open to you. If you need me, call, and I'll be here." He waited a moment, and then another, so his parents could respond if they wished to.

"Okay," he said when they remained silent. "I love you. Talk to you later."

He'd taken a couple of steps back into the house when his mother said, "We love you too, Zach."

"Joan," his father said as the door closed. "Enough."

Sadness pulled through Zach, but he kept walking. He got in the truck with Paul, determined now.

"How'd it go?" his son asked.

"Not well." Zach looked out the window, watching as Paul drove down the lane to the road.

"Home?" Paul asked.

"No," Zach said, an idea coming to him. "Go straight across to that farm. I want to talk to Celia's brothers."

CHAPTER 21

C elia measured and mixed, baking off each layer of the cake to exact perfection. After all, this was her daughter, and she deserved a flawless wedding cake.

The dress was ready. The décor. The refreshments. The venue. They'd managed to work together and check all the boxes in anticipation of Reagan and Dale's union.

Celia wept as she whipped buttercream for the inner frosting, her thoughts first revolving around Brandon. They'd lived in this house together for only two years before he'd died. He'd filled it with laughter and love in that time, but the sound of those chuckles didn't exist in Celia's memory anymore.

She couldn't remember what he smelled like, or what he might say on a day like today. She'd spent so much time missing him, and she almost felt like her whole life had passed her by while she'd thought about him, knitted sweaters for her dogs, and poured her time and energy into her girls.

None of those were bad things, but Zach had opened her eyes to the fact that her life could be so much more. *She* was so much more.

She glanced at the phone sitting on the counter, silent. It had been three days, and he still hadn't called or texted. Not even once. She'd expected him to, and each minute felt like a stab to the heart now.

His message—unsent and unspoken as it was—had come through loud and clear. He wasn't interested in a relationship with her. Or, perhaps he was, but not at the price he had to pay to have it.

The phone rang, and she jumped out of her skin. Her heart pounded against her breastbone, the hope ballooning into a very real and very tangible thing. She hated that she still held such hope that Zach would call.

And hated even more that Ophelia's name sat on the screen. "Hey, O," she said after she'd swiped open the call. She sounded chipper and bright, just as she wanted to.

"What time do you girls want me to come over to do the makeup on Sunday?"

"Oh, let's see," Celia said, thinking. "The wedding is at two. Reagan's hairdresser is coming at ten. How about eleven? I'll feed you lunch."

"Eleven it is," Ophelia said. "And Celia, you're not feeding me. I already have brisket smoking. I'll bring lunch on Sunday. You have enough going on."

"It's okay. I can—"

"And Larissa is coming," Ophelia said.

Celia paused. "She is? Is she...?"

"She and Mack went to counseling this week," Ophelia said. "I just know they're going to be able to work things out."

"I hope so," Celia said. "I'll add them to my prayers." She'd been praying for her brother anyway, but Larissa deserved some of Celia's time on her knees too.

"How are you holding up?"

Celia opened her mouth to say she was fine. Okay. Doing great. But they were all false, and she knew it. "The wedding prep is stressful," she said instead. "But we'll make it." And then she'd be alone again.

Reagan and Dale would move to Ohio. Ruth spent most of her time at work, or out with Grizz, or down in Cheyenne, visiting her boyfriend. Celia didn't want her to do anything different, but the loneliness that plagued her now seemed twice as sharp as it had been before she'd started dating Zach.

"I meant how are you holding up doing this all by yourself?"

"I mean, what choice do I have?" Celia asked, too much bite in the question. "I'm sorry, Ophelia. I'm just...tired."

"You don't need to apologize to me."

Celia had lived much of her life using the question *what choice do I have?* Brandon had died. She couldn't bring him back.

Zach had made his choice. She couldn't make him call her.

"I have to go," she said, her voice tight and choked. "The timer on my cake is going off." She hung up before Ophelia could argue or realize there was no timer sounding. Her tears started anew, but this time, they belonged to Zach and not Brandon.

"It's so beautiful outside," Ruth said, practically breathless as she came in with Grizz on a leash. The dog's tongue hung out of his mouth, but he came right over to Celia and looked up at her with that signature Labrador smile on his face.

"Hey, boy," she said, taking the excuse to bury her face in the scruff of his neck to hide her tears from her daughter. "Did you have a good walk with Auntie Ruthie?"

The timer on the cakes in the oven did go off then, and she used that distraction to turn away from Ruth. She'd managed to compose herself by the time she had to turn around, and she wiped her hair out of her eyes with the back of her hand.

"All right. Only a few cakes left."

"Mom," Ruth said.

"Hmm?"

"He hasn't called, has he?"

Celia's emotions sprang right back into her throat, stinging her. She shook her head and started measuring out the cake batter she needed for the next tier of cakes, spreading the batter evenly into the two twelve-inch-round cake pans.

As soon as she slid them into the oven and turned around, Ruth wrapped her arms around Celia. "I'm sorry, Mom."

Celia clung to her, not wanting her daughter to know how weak she was, but needing someone to anchor herself to.

"I'm sorry," she said a few moments later. She tried to step back, but Ruth held her tight. "I'm okay, really."

Ruth released her, and Celia wiped at her face. "The wedding is in two days. We'll get through this, and everything will be fine."

Her daughter looked dubious, but she didn't say anything. She glanced around the kitchen, which admittedly looked like a war zone, if the weapons were flour, frosting, and frothy egg whites.

"All right," Ruth said. "Tell me what needs to be done."

❦

THAT EVENING, all of the cakes had been baked, wrapped, and placed in the freezer. Celia would trim, frost, and decorate the cake tomorrow. It was the last thing that needed to be done for the wedding.

She lay on the couch, her feet up in front of her on the ottoman, sandwiched between her daughters. Dale had crowded onto the couch too, his arm around Reagan, as they all watched a romantic comedy together.

Happiness filtered through Celia. She did love her girls, and they had always been enough for her. Perhaps they would be again. Or maybe she could start dating someone else. Amanda had been out with several older men in the area.

The idea felt absolutely wrong, though, and Celia knew why. She'd given her heart to that cowboy up in Dog Valley, and until she figured out how to get it back, she wouldn't be setting up any more dates.

Although, Reagan was getting married, and maybe there'd be another best man there for her....

She dismissed the idea. Dale was almost thirty, not almost fifty, and he wouldn't have anyone acting as best man that would be age-appropriate for Celia.

She didn't want anyone else anyway.

She wanted her sexy, salty-haired, cowboy billionaire best man from Saltgrass Farms. A sigh came out of her mouth as the hero and heroine on-screen finally kissed, and Ruth slipped her fingers into Celia's.

Celia squeezed her daughter's hand and sat up. Her back ached, and her head pounded, and it was definitely time for her old bones to get to bed. "Okay, girls," she said. "I'm going to bed."

"It's not even eight-thirty yet," Reagan said.

"And I baked today for eight hours," Celia said with a smile. She leaned down and swept a kiss across her daughter's forehead. "I'm tired."

"You can't go to bed yet," Reagan said, a panicked look crossing her face.

"Why not? Dale can stay, Rae." She looked at Ruth, who also wore a puzzled look in her eyes.

Reagan opened her mouth to say something, but only stammering came out. "It's just...maybe you could make us some of that butterscotch popcorn before you go to bed."

"Really, Rae?" Ruth asked. "You're going to ask her to do more cooking for you?" She stood up and went behind the couch. "Come on, Mom. If you want to go to bed, go to bed. I'll let Grizz out for you."

Celia's already raw feelings felt pinched. "I can take him out." She took the leash from Ruth and clipped it to Grizz's collar. "Come on, bud." She went out the front door, because none of her property was fenced anyway.

Behind her, she heard Ruth and Reagan start to talk, but she didn't stay to see what they were arguing about. It didn't matter. Whatever it was would wash out, just like all of their disagreements had.

If only Zach could get his family's disagreements with hers to wash away. Just float down the river.

"Go potty," she told the dog, and Grizz started to sniff around, looking for the just-right spot.

It was a beautiful night, following the beautiful day Ruth had spoken of earlier. June would arrive next week, and summer would fully arrive in Coral Canyon. Finally.

Winter had been very long this year, though Celia had barely had any time to be disgruntled about it. Everything seemed to make her disgruntled now.

Grizz finished, and just as he came back over to her, a pair of headlights cut through the gathering twilight on Celia's street. She automatically shied away from the advancing truck, backing up toward the front steps as it came closer and closer.

They'd go right past, as her brothers would've told her if they were coming over tonight.

But the truck turned into her driveway. Grizz laid down at her feet, utterly unconcerned about this unexpected visitor.

Besides, she knew that truck.

Knew the man who unfolded himself from the driver's seat and came around the front of the vehicle.

Owen Zuckerman.

Celia's heartbeat rippled like a flag in a stiff wind, but before she could say anything, another truck turned the corner and came toward them. This truck pulled in right behind Owen, and Mack got out of the passenger side while Lennox emerged from the driver's side.

"What is going on?" she demanded, feeling braver now that her brothers were here.

"Just a second, Celia," Lennox said, turning to look over his shoulder.

Sure enough, a third truck—really, her driveway was full enough—turned and drove toward them.

Her breath caught somewhere inside her body when she recognized this one. "Zach," she whispered, her eyes glued to the windshield.

"See?" Mack said somewhere outside her awareness. "She loves him. How can you keep them apart?"

The third truck pulled in, but it wasn't Zack driving. Instead, Celia found his son, Paul. Frantic to see Zach now, she took a step forward, freezing as the passenger door opened, and Zach got out.

Their eyes met, and Celia could barely breathe. He wore his regular jeans, cowboy boots, a plain old blue T-shirt, and that hat she'd seen months ago at Amanda's wedding.

He was nothing special, but so sexy, and so absolutely special *to her* that she couldn't move.

"Celia," he said, and his voice fixed everything. "Wondering if you had a few minutes to talk."

She couldn't look away from him, though there were three other cowboys gathered on her front sidewalk. "I—"

"Say yes, Mom," Reagan called from behind her, and Celia turned. She hadn't even noticed her daughter opening the front door.

She swung her attention back to Zach, and he'd advanced several steps closer to her. So close, she could smell his cologne and see the light from her porch lamp in the dark depths of his eyes.

"I guess I have a minute to talk," Celia said, and Zach's lips curved into a slow, sexy smile.

"Great."

CHAPTER 22

Zach stared at Celia, his mouth suddenly stuffed with cotton. He'd thought bringing reinforcements would make things easier, but now, with everyone watching, he realized he'd made a huge mistake.

"Say something," Mack said out of the corner of his mouth.

Zach cleared his throat and tugged at the collar on his shirt. "So it took me a few days to get everyone on the same page." He looked at his brother.

Owen still wasn't quite on the same page as Zach, but he'd come. He'd talked to Mack and Lennox yesterday. Zach had hope the two families could work through their problems for the first time in his life.

"My dad is still completely against us being together," he said. "But I'm in love with you, and I want to be with you."

Celia lifted one hand up to her throat, and pressed her

palm against her chest. She was so beautiful, and Zach couldn't believe he'd even considered walking away from her simply because his dad said to.

"I know I'm not perfect," he said. "But Owen is willing to let go of the past."

"I'm willing to try," Owen clarified.

"And so are we," Mack said. "Right, Lennox?"

"I've wanted to find peace with the Zuckermans for years," Lennox said. "I'm all for this."

"Owen?" Zach prompted.

His brother low-key glared at him, but Zach held his ground. Owen finally looked at Celia, and he visibly softened. She really had that effect on people, because she was so good.

Zach's emotions spiraled up and then down. She had to take him back. He'd fixed things for them. No, they wouldn't be perfect, but it was a start. Someone had to take the first step, and Zach was willing to do it. He'd been praying she would be too.

"Celia," Owen said. "I realize my hard feelings are not for you, or Zach for that matter. He seems to have already given up his heart." He cleared his throat, obviously as uncomfortable as Zach. "And he's my brother, and I want him to be happy."

Zach clapped his hand on his brother's shoulder, his gratitude multiplying. The Lord had really answered his prayers this week. Maybe not exactly how he wanted them answered, but he was here. Making things right.

Zach looked at Celia again. "So?" he asked. "What do

you think?"

Thanks to it almost being June, there was still plenty of light left in the day to illuminate her face. Her eyes held an edge of fear. Maybe determination.

"Come on, Celia," Mack said, and Zach hadn't known he'd have to be the prompter in this conversation.

"Are you sure?" she asked.

"As sure as I've ever been," Zach said. "About anything."

"You'll have to move to Dog Valley," Reagan said, joining her mother at the bottom of the porch steps.

"I—that's okay," Celia said. "Zach has a beautiful farm there."

"I know, Mom." Reagan smiled at her mother as Ruth came down the steps too. "You've told us all about it."

"You're all she ever talks about," Ruth added, and Zach smiled.

"Oh, stop it," Celia said. "He is not."

"Then get over there and kiss him," Reagan said, giving Celia a little nudge.

She walked toward him, and the look in her eye was definitely made of something positive. She reached up and took his face in both of her hands. Tipping up on her toes, she whispered, "I love you, but I'm not kissing you in front of everyone."

"Let's go for a walk then," he said.

She settled onto her feet, turned and picked up the leash for Grizz, and said, "I'll be back in a little bit."

"Not so tired now, are you?" Reagan asked.

"Ignore her," Celia said, rolling her eyes. Instead of coming back to Zach's side, she handed him Grizz's leash and stepped over to Mack.

They hugged, and Mack said clearly, "You've waited a long time for a man like him."

She embraced Lennox too, who said something Zach couldn't hear. He wasn't sure he was anything special, but he wanted to be. For Celia, he'd try.

A hint of nerves skipped across her face as she went to Owen. Zach thought she'd shake his hand, but she moved right in and hugged him too.

"I'm looking forward to getting to know you, Owen," she said.

His big, gruff older brother hugged her back and said, "Me too, Celia."

Happiness like Zach had never known moved through him, and he turned to Paul. "You can wait a little bit?"

"We're just putting on another movie," Reagan said. "You're welcome to come in."

"Take your time, Dad." Paul stepped past him and grinned at Celia. "Good to see you again, Celia."

Celia smiled at him and threaded her fingers through Zach's. He held very still as the other men got back in their trucks and backed out of her driveway.

And then he was finally alone with her. Their eyes met, and Zach exhaled a nervous chuckle. "I meant every word I said."

"I know," Celia said. "You aren't one to say something and not mean it."

"They didn't get to decide," he said. "I chose. I chose *you.*"

She beamed up at him. "And I choose you."

Finally, Zach gathered her into his arms and leaned down and touched his lips to hers in a sweet kiss with the woman he loved.

※

"TELL me how that little meeting happened," she said as they strolled down the sidewalk to the corner. Grizz didn't seem keen on going much faster, and Zach didn't blame him. He hadn't exactly been sleeping super well this week.

"I went to see my dad again," Zach said. "He is set in his ways. Stubborn. He would not give an inch. But my mother said she loved me, and when Paul got to the end of the road, I told him to go straight."

"To my brothers' place."

"They weren't home, but I talked to your sister-in-law, and she called Lennox on the radio."

"Mm," Celia said. "And?"

"And they were surprised, but at least they're completely open to the idea of moving on." He squeezed her hand. "I mean, I knew they would be. You've said that. But I basically asked them what I should do. Mack could see I was miserable, and he said I needed to appeal to Owen, not my father."

Zach could still feel that slip of misery move through him as he sat at the dining room table in Lennox's house.

"So I went back across the street, and I talked to my brother. He loves his wife."

Celia paused as Grizz found something to sniff. "Why does that matter?"

"I appealed to that side of him," Zach said. "And he does want me to be happy, and he said he couldn't imagine his life without Aleah."

Zach lifted Celia's hand to his lips. "I hope I'm not too late to RSVP to the wedding."

"Do you even have anything to wear? It's in one day."

"I can make it happen," he said. "I'd been planning to come."

"Good," she said, her voice wobbling a little bit. "Because I really don't want to do this by myself anymore."

Compassion hit Zach right in his heart. "I know, Celia. And now you don't have to." Regret came next. "I'm sorry I've been gone these past couple of weeks. What do you need help with to be ready for Sunday?"

"I'm making the cake tomorrow," she said. "I could use someone to sit by me as I put it all together."

"Company," he said. "I can do that." He lifted his hurt hand. "I don't do a whole lot around the farm at the moment."

"Is Paul helping?"

"Doing most of it," he said. "And working online. He's a great kid." Pride filled Zach. "And he's changed his major to computer science."

"I can't wait to meet your daughters," Celia said.

"Me either," Zach said. "I should plan something for us." He thought about Abby in D.C. She'd come, and maybe she'd bring Michael.

Zach started telling Celia about the man his second daughter was seeing, and the conversation was so easy and so amazing after a couple of weeks with only himself for company.

By the time he and Paul pulled into Saltgrass Farm, it was much too late and Zach's throat was beyond dry from all the talking he'd been doing.

But every word and every sentence had been worth it.

"I'm going to look at airplane tickets," Paul said as his phone went off. "Lindsey just said she could come for the Fourth."

"Really?" Zach had let his son run with the planning of a family reunion so everyone could meet Celia.

"I need to talk to Celia before we start booking plane tickets," he said. "What did Abby say about Michael?"

"He's talking to his work on Monday."

"So we have a few days to wait."

"Yeah," Paul said, parking. "You don't want to do it?"

"Of course I do," Zach said. "We could rent cabins or something and spend some time out in the Tetons. Remember we did that one year? Float the river. Ride the boat at Jenny Lake. Go up to the top of the world on the gondola."

"Some places book out a year in advance," Paul said. "You might not be able to get cabins, but I'm sure there's a hotel."

"We could go to the Bar J Wranglers," Zach said, all of the activities coming together in his mind.

"Who's getting ahead of himself now?" Paul laughed, and they walked into the house together.

Ginger and Maple met them, tails wagging, and Zach bent down to greet his dogs. "It went great, guys," he said. "She'll come live with us soon." He straightened and looked at Paul. "I'll wait to ask her about the Fourth after the wedding. She's swamped right now."

"Ah, I see." Paul nodded and opened the fridge. The kid could drink soda at any hour, and Zach didn't understand it. He'd had a cola at eight last night and been up for hours with heartburn.

Or maybe that had been anxiety over talking to Celia tonight, or what Owen would say. He hadn't been fully on-board with Zach's plan until this morning.

"I hope it works out for the Fourth," Paul said. "It will be fun to meet Abby's boyfriend."

"Right?" Zach grinned at his son and pulled him into a hug. "Thank you for everything you've done for me this week. I'm so glad you're here."

"Me too, Dad." Paul grinned at him. "You headed to bed?"

"Is it that obvious that I'm exhausted?"

"Yes." Paul laughed, and Zach did too. He did head down the hall to his bedroom after that, closing the door, and immediately falling to his knees to thank the Lord for bringing Celia back into his life.

CHAPTER 23

C elia woke on Sunday morning when Grizz licked
her face. "All right," she said, laughing as she
pushed the pup away. When he got right in her
face, he needed to go out, and she got up to let him into
the backyard.

She stood at the sliding glass door, the morning light
filling the sky as Grizz sniffed around. With his business
taken care of, he came back in, tail wagging.

She fed him and put out fresh water before her eyes
caught on the wedding cake. She'd finished it yesterday,
with Zach sitting at the bar while she worked on getting
every fondant rose where it belonged.

The cake was beautiful and elegant, with a soft while
background on the five tiers. Then Celia had done roses in
Reagan's wedding colors, and added the edible flowers
she'd ordered in from Cheyenne.

Tears pricked her eyes. She couldn't believe her

daughter was getting married today. Couldn't believe Reagan was old enough to do something so grown up. And Celia couldn't believe *she* was old enough to have a daughter getting married.

Not only that, but she had her boyfriend back. Her best friend. Her anchor. "Wish you were here, Brandon," she whispered, touching two fingers to her lips and then touching the silver plate that held the cake.

Sure, she missed him. She'd always miss him and wish he was there to witness the major events of their children's lives.

But she also had a wonderful future ahead of her with Zach Zuckerman.

Now that she was awake, she wouldn't be going back to sleep, though Grizz trotted back into the bedroom and jumped up onto the bed.

Celia collected her phone and went out into the living room. She enjoyed the early-morning silence, and she must have dozed at some point, because Ruth woke her with the words, "Mom, it's time to start getting ready for the wedding."

Celia sat up, her brain foggy—until she looked at the clock. "Oh, my goodness." She jumped to her feet. "I'm going to shower. Where's Reagan?"

"Already out," Ruth said. "I've showered too. Coffee's on in the kitchen. Claudia will be here to start on Reagan's hair soon."

Celia nodded and hurried down the hall. While Reagan got mostly ready here, Ruth and Celia would go over to the reception center and get all the tables decorated. The bigger items they'd rented—the altar, an arch, and a few other things—would be brought by the designer, and they were meeting at noon, as soon as their rental began.

When she came out in her mother-of-the-bride dress, her hair styled perfectly, she stalled at the sight of Zach standing in her living room.

He wore a black suit that looked brand new. He'd told her he was going shopping yesterday, but then he'd spent most of the day in her kitchen, so she wasn't sure when he'd purchased that suit.

It hardly mattered. His shoulders filled out the jacket nicely, and with that hat? Celia's heart stalled completely for a few breaths.

"Hey, beautiful," he said, his voice so sexy it reached right into her soul and filled her with light.

"When did you get here?" she asked, moving toward him and making his suit jacket lay flat though it already was.

"Just a minute ago," he said, taking her effortlessly into his arms. Everything about him appealed to her, and she was so glad she'd been at the lodge for Amanda's wedding, though she never would've missed it.

He kissed her, and Celia lost herself to the touch and taste of him.

"Hey," Reagan said. "Stop kissing." She laughed, and Celia ducked her head, slightly embarrassed.

"I can't wait for her to get married," Celia said.

Zach chuckled, and Celia pressed her cheek right

against the sound of it in his chest. "Where do you need me?" he asked.

"Right here," she said, stepping back. "I'm just getting my makeup done, and then I'll use our muscles at the reception center."

"Okay," he said. "So I'll sit here by Grizz until we're ready to go?"

"Yep."

Celia went with Reagan and sat in the chair Ophelia told her to. She kept her eyes closed and her voice low as she told Ophelia all about the situation from Friday night.

"Lennox was so happy when he got home," Ophelia said, brushing something on Celia's cheeks. "I'm thrilled for you, obviously. When will you two get married?"

Celia's heartbeat doubled for a few beats. "Oh, I don't know. We've only been dating a few months."

"I hear Christmas is a great time."

"That's only a few months."

"It's *seven* months, Mom," Ruth said. "And you put this wedding together in just over two. You'd be fine."

"A Christmas wedding," Celia mused, her mind moving through ideas now. She didn't want to get married at the lodge the way Amanda had. But she didn't want something like Reagan, at a more formal venue.

She wanted something at Saltgrass Farm, the idea popping into her head. But the best time of year for that would be summer—and it was already summer.

Ophelia started talking about Larissa and Mack, and

Celia just let her talk. Apparently things were going well, and Celia let the joyful light move through her.

"Okay," Ophelia finally said. "You're done. As soon as I finish with Reagan, I'll go get Mama and bring her over."

"Thanks," Celia said. "Ruth, let's get loaded up and get going."

Zach came with them, and time slipped away like smoke. Before she knew it, guests started arriving, and she hooked her arm through her mother's and led her to the front row.

"Right here, Ma."

"I want to meet your man," she said, her voice practically filling the whole hall.

Celia grinned at her, only a slip of embarrassment heating her cheeks. "Let me grab him for you."

But he wasn't anywhere to be found. "Have you seen Zach?" she asked Ruth.

"Nope."

She asked Mack and Lennox, and no one had seen him. Confused, she finally pulled out her phone. She needed to get back to Reagan and make sure the veil was right and her daughter was ready to walk down the aisle.

Dale's brother was walking Reagan down the aisle, and Celia wanted to watch her every step.

She started toward the bride's room as the call to Zach connected. She heard his phone ring, and more confusion than ever filled her. She paused in the hall, turning until she could tell where the sound came from.

She pushed open the room where Reagan would be, and Zach was there too.

"It's your mom," he said, his back to her.

"She's right behind you," Reagan said.

Zach spun toward her, and she lowered her phone. "What's going on here?" she asked, looking from Zach to Reagan.

"I asked him to walk me down the aisle," Reagan said, a huge smile on her face. "He said yes, and I'm just giving him some directions."

"I'm scared out of my mind," Zach said. "I'm not ready for this."

"Sure you are," Reagan said. "You just don't let me fall." She stepped into her heels, wobbling like she'd break her ankle and fall down in the next moment.

Zach must've thought so too, because he lunged toward her and grabbed onto her arm.

"See?" Reagan beamed up at him. "You're doing great." She tippy-toed toward Celia. "Do you want a picture, Mom?"

Celia worked hard to keep the tears from streaming down her face. Ophelia's masterful makeup would be ruined. Her hands trembled as she tried to pull up her camera.

"Mom," Reagan said. "It's okay."

"I'm okay," Celia said, though she felt moments away from bursting into tears. Big, fat tears that would ruin everything. "Almost got it."

The camera finally came up and she took a quick

picture of two of her favorite people, her heart filled with love.

"Now go on," Reagan said. "I don't want to be late to my own wedding, and we can't start until you sit down." She grinned, her own eyes watery.

Celia couldn't leave without hugging her daughter, and she ended up embracing Zach too, the three of them clinging to each other for a few precious moments.

"Okay," she said, fixing the top of her dress. "Okay, I'm fine. I am." She turned and left the bride's room and went back into the grand hall. She felt so many eyes on her as she moved down the aisle, and she squeezed Amanda's hand as she went by.

"They're coming," she said to her mother. "The man walking Reagan down the aisle is mine."

And oh, how she loved saying that.

THE NEXT MORNING DAWNED QUIETLY. Reagan and Dale were gone, off on their honeymoon in California. Then they'd be in Ohio, and Dale would start his new job.

Celia sat on the front steps, watching Grizz chase the birds in the yard. Ruth came outside and sat beside her, leaning her head against Celia's shoulder.

"It was a beautiful wedding."

"It was."

Several moments of silence passed, and then Ruth

asked, "Do you think Zach would walk me down the aisle when I marry Brandon?"

Celia's breath stuck in her lungs. "I don't know which thing to address first," she said.

"He hasn't asked me yet, but we've started talking about marriage," Ruth said.

"You're not done with college."

"That's not a requirement to get married, Mom," Ruth said with a smile. "And Brandon's almost done. He's a few years older than me."

Celia thought of Ruth leaving as well, and while the thought pinched, she knew it was right. She'd known she wouldn't have her daughters forever.

"Would you get married by Christmas?" she asked.

"Probably not," Ruth said. "That's open for you, Mom, if you want it."

"Zach and I haven't even talked about marriage." Celia watched Grizz roll around in the grass, obviously enjoying himself.

"He's thought about it," Ruth said. "Even if he hasn't said anything."

"Maybe," Celia said.

"Is he coming over today?"

"No," Celia said. "Graham gave me the day off, and I'm not going to Dog Valley until tomorrow." She sighed, enjoying the peaceful nature of this neighborhood. She'd miss this road. This house. The sense of community she felt here.

She'd feel all of that in Dog Valley, she knew. Finn and

Celia still went to church down here, but she and Zach hadn't talked about that either.

She suddenly felt very ill-equipped to be merging her life with another human's.

It's Zach, she told herself. And she loved him. He loved her. Which meant everything would work out.

CHAPTER 24

Zach pushed the cart around the grocery store, whistling as he put hot dog buns in the basket. Then hamburger buns. Then more condiments than one man should need.

But he wasn't just one man. All of his kids were coming for the Fourth of July. He had a boat tour booked for Jenny Lake, but they'd just drive the forty minutes to the lake and stay at his farm the other days.

Paul had bought a volleyball net and set it up in the backyard, though Zach had said they didn't have enough people for volleyball.

Paul said two-on-two worked just fine, and since Abby was bringing Michael, they had enough.

He'd broken up with his girlfriend, and Lindsey hadn't been seeing anyone in a while now. Zach was just excited to have them all with him for several days—and for them to meet Celia.

She was bringing Ruth and Brandon, and Zach went down the cookie aisle to make sure to get the lemon sandwich cookies Celia's daughter liked so much.

By the time he left the grocery store, he'd spent hundreds and ran back in three times for things he'd forgotten. He sat in the cab of his truck and texted Celia.

What else do we need?

Are you still at the grocery store?

Yes, and I don't want to come back. I've run in three times already.

Celia started listing things she needed, and Zach had gotten them all.

I think we're good then, she said. *Paul's out with the horses and then he's leaving for the airport, so I'll help you haul it all in when you get back.*

Zach drove through an ice cream shop to get a twist cone, and then he inched down the quiet streets of Dog Valley, enjoying this place where he lived. He'd like it a whole lot more when Celia would be at the farm permanently.

They'd talked a little bit about getting married in the five weeks since her daughter's wedding. Nothing too serious, and he didn't really know when or where she'd like to get married.

But he'd bought a ring a week ago, and he kept it in the box on top of his dresser. If the opportunity presented itself, he'd decided he'd ask. See what she said.

He pulled into the driveway, Paul's truck gone. He'd been designated as the airport taxi, and everyone was arriving in Jackson within a half an hour of each other today.

"Paul finished with the horses?" he asked.

"He left five minutes ago," Celia said, reaching for a bag of groceries in the back of the truck. "I'm surprised you didn't see him on the road."

"I might have stopped for an ice cream cone on the way home."

Celia burst out laughing. "I'm not surprised." She grinned at him and together, they hauled in the groceries.

"I think you bought the whole store, Zach," she teased. "This is ridiculous." She started unpacking the groceries and putting them away in his cupboards and fridge as if she lived there.

"Celia," he said, watching her. He opened his mouth to say something else, but he honestly didn't know what.

"Hmm?" She finally paused when he remained silent and looked at him.

His emotions kept him silent for another few seconds. "I've been thinking about marrying you."

A sparkle entered her eyes. "Oh?"

"Yeah," he said. "We haven't talked about it much, but I'm wondering what you think."

She turned and put a handful of cold cuts in the fridge, hiding her face from him. "I think it's a good idea."

"I want you here at the farm with me," he said, coming around the island.

"I'm still going to work at the lodge."

"I know," he said. "But you don't have to if you don't want to."

"I want to. I love those boys." She faced him again.

He nodded, knowing she did.

"And they have a huge Christmas tradition up at the lodge. I love going, and I want you to come too."

"I know," he said. "You've already told me not to make plans for Christmas Eve, or if I do, that the kids have to come up to the lodge for the tree lighting."

She nodded. "Yep, that's right."

Zach wanted to get back on-topic. "Do we want a fancy wedding? What are you thinking? Have you thought about it at all?"

"Oh, I've thought about it," she said, abandoning the groceries to just converse with him. "I would like to get married right here, at Saltgrass Farms."

His eyebrows shot up. "Really?"

"Really." She smiled up at him. "In that beautiful back-yard you have. With all our kids here. And the Whittaker boys. And Finn and Amanda. And maybe a few of my friends from Coral Canyon."

"Deal," he said. "When?"

"When does it snow here?"

"Depends on how cruel Mother Nature is," he said. "But usually by Halloween."

"Three months," Celia said. "Are we ready for that?"

Zach took her into his arms, his desire for her roaring through him. "I'm ready for that." He touched his lips to hers, gently, exploring. She kissed him back with enthusiasm, and Zach thought she was ready too.

Celia pulled away, and they breathed together. That simple gesture, that easy motion, reminded Zach of how wonderful life could be with a companion.

"All right," she said. "I think Ruth will be engaged soon as well. Maybe we should put a date on the calendar."

"Hold that thought." Zach jogged into his bedroom to snatch the ring box from his dresser. He returned to the kitchen much slower than he'd left it, his heart beating double-time in his chest. "I bought this last week." He cracked the lid, and it seemed like last time he'd proposed had been so much more romantic.

He'd definitely planned things better.

"Zach," Celia breathed, her hands going to her mouth.

"I love you," he said, the best speech he could come up with on such short notice. "Will you marry me?"

Her eyes shone with happiness, and she nodded. Zach realized he hadn't even gotten down on one knee. Probably for the best, as he was old now, and he might not be able to get back up.

"And you still think you want to live here at Saltgrass Farm?" he asked, taking the ring out of the silk inside the box with trembling fingers.

"Yes," she said, her voice strong. She held out her hand, and he slid the ring onto it.

"Looks like it needs to be sized," he said, meeting her eyes.

A tremor of fear lived there, and he bent down and kissed her. "What's wrong?"

"It's going to be hard for me to leave that house."

"Then don't leave it," he said. "I can come live down there. You have a little bit of land. Enough for the four horses I have."

Tears brimmed in her eyes, and she shook her head. "No, it's time."

"Maybe one of your girls would want it," he said. "Like how Eli moved into Amanda's house."

She tucked herself against his chest, her tears hot as they stained his shirt. "No," she said. "They won't. Ruth's Brandon will take her far from here, same as Dale and Reagan."

Zach detected the sadness in Celia's voice, and he understood it on a deeper level than he cared to admit. "Then we'll just have them back to the farm as often as we can," he said. "The way the Whittakers get together at Christmas."

"I'd like that," she said, straightening. She looked down at her hand and then up at him. "I'm going to need help going through that house. Will you come help me with it?"

"There's nothing I'd like more." He smiled down at her, gratitude that God had prompted him to get to Finn's wedding, even though he hadn't wanted to go. He brought her close to him again, swaying with her into a dance. "Can we dance at our wedding?" he murmured.

"Sure," she whispered back. "Just put down a floor in that barn, and we'll be set to go."

🪷

A COUPLE OF HOURS LATER, Zach stood in front of the grill as smoke lifted into the air above his head.

"They're here," Celia said, her voice bursting out onto the deck at the same time she did. He turned immediately from the grill and hurried inside, securing her hand in his. He hadn't been nervous until that very moment.

"I'm not going to be able to talk to her," Celia said, her grip much too tight to be comfortable.

"It's fine," Zach told her for the tenth time. She'd started to learn a little sign language so she could communicate with Abby, but Zach knew there was nothing better than being thrown in the fire when it came to learning a new language. "Abby talks to people all the time who can't sign."

Before he could say anything else, the garage door opened, and laughter filled the space. Paul entered first, almost backward, his hands flying through signs.

"He says Abby better talk to me about that first," Zach said. "Talk to me about what?" He let go of her hand as he moved forward, his hands moving through the motions. He was much slower than Paul, and Abby didn't answer.

Her whole face lit up, and she threw herself into his arms with a strangled "Dad," coming from her mouth.

Everything inside Zach felt zipped tight as he hugged

his daughter. Oh, how he loved her, and it was so nice to have her with him, safe and sound and whole and well.

"Hey, baby," he said, though she wouldn't be able to hear him. He'd told her once, long ago, that he'd always greet her with a hug and those words, and she'd feel the vibrations from her chest to his as he spoke and know what she'd said.

"Daddy," Lindsey said, though she was the oldest. She abandoned her suitcase just inside the door, tears flowing down her face as she joined the embrace. Zach held them both tight, trying not to let his own tears out.

Paul continued to talk and sign as he moved into the kitchen, Abby's boyfriend with him.

Zach finally cleared his throat. "Girls," he said, stepping back and making the sign for Abby. "This is my fiancée, Celia Armstrong." He started to spell out her name, but no one was watching him.

"Fiancée?" Paul practically bellowed. "Dad, what did you do while I was gone?"

Lindsey squealed and danced over to Celia, who hugged her with a big smile. She showed the ring to her, and they both turned back to Zach and Abby.

Celia looked like she'd swallowed snakes and they were about to make a reappearance. But she made the few signs Zach had taught her—*Abby, so nice to meet you.*

Abby's hands flashed like lightning, and Paul laughed again. "Abs, you have to slow down. I can't even keep up with you." He watched her again, and even Zach caught the meaning this time.

"She says you need a sign for your name," Paul said. "Abby doesn't like to spell anything out." He grinned at her, and she rolled her eyes.

"Oh, uh," Celia said, looking at him for help.

"You do it, Abby," Zach said, signing as he spoke. "And you haven't even introduced your boyfriend yet."

Her fingers and hands and arms moved, and Zach laughed. "Fair enough. I did spring fiancée on you." He stepped over to Celia and put his arm around her. "Time to meet the boyfriend."

For some reason, his stomach clenched as he faced Michael for truly the first time. He was tall, easily six or seven inches taller than Abby, with dark hair and bright, brown eyes. He wore a smile with his red and white checkered shirt and jeans, and Zach thought he put off a good air.

"Dad, this is Michael Farmer," he narrated for Celia as Abby spoke. "Michael, my father." She beamed at both of them, and Zach stepped over to the other man, speaking to him with his hands. They shook hands, and Michael asked Zach when he'd gotten engaged.

"He asked when we got engaged," Zach said with a laugh. "You tell him. This is how you say today." He showed her the sign, and Celia performed it for Michael, a timid smile on her face. They shook hands too, and Zach turned her toward Lindsey.

"My oldest," he said. "Lindsey."

"I've heard so much about you all," Celia said, giving

Lindsey and Abby a quick hug each. Zach signed for her, and Abby waved her hand when Celia stepped back.

"She's got the perfect sign for you," Zach said. "This is going to be good." He grinned at his daughter. "Make it fast, Abs. I need to get the meat on the grill."

She looked like she'd just won the lottery. She made her right hand into a C-shape and pushed it straight up. Two pumps. "Celia," he said, still reading Abby's hands. "Like ceiling, but so much better."

"I should hope I'm better than a ceiling," Celia said. "Just wait until you taste the potato salad. Then you'll think so."

Zach, Lindsey, and Paul laughed, and as Paul finished signing for Celia, so did Michael and Abby.

Zach's heart had never been so full. He loved these people with all of his heart, and he stepped over to the counter. "Okay, meat." He started for the back door, watching as Abby seamlessly stepped into Michael's arms and kissed him.

Joy touched his heart, and he thanked God for amazing children in his life. He started putting burgers on the grill, and Celia joined him a moment later.

"They'll be engaged soon too," Celia said, leaning into him. "They're clearly in love with each other, and I didn't even have to ask them to know it."

"I agree," Zach said, glancing over his shoulder. "I hope Lindsey takes it okay. She's always been protective of Abby, and she's always felt second to her."

"I'll watch the burgers," Celia said. "If you want to go talk to her."

"I'll give her a minute," Zach said, because he didn't want to be anywhere but where he currently was: at his fiancée's side.

CHAPTER 25

Celia woke one morning and realized summer was gone. She didn't know quite where it had gone, but between cleaning out her house, listing it for sale, and planning her own wedding, the hours, days, and months had disappeared.

Today, she was moving and getting married in the same day. The house had sold two weeks ago, and the Whittaker boys would be in front of her house in an hour.

She'd promised them all blueberry muffins and hot coffee if they'd come help her move. Graham had taken her into a bear hug and said, "Celia, you don't have to bribe me to get me there. I wouldn't miss it."

And she knew he wouldn't. In fact, he'd arranged to pick up the truck, and he'd called a few cowboy friends to come help. She'd insisted she didn't have much, but as she took one more walk around her house, she realized she did.

Zach's house had everything someone needed to live, so some of her things were going in his storage shed in the backyard. Amanda had told her it would be hard to leave her home, and while Celia had been anticipating it, the full weight of the idea hadn't hit her until now.

Amanda had also told her it would be hard to simply move into Zach's house and think of it as hers. It was more than just taking her clothes and toiletries. She needed to make his house hers, so she'd packed her decorations and was bringing them. Her own linens, towels, pots and pans, and knick knacks.

She'd cleared it with the new owners to leave a few pieces of furniture, but Brandon's desk was coming with her, and Zach had assured her many times that he had a spot for it in his library. She was taking the beds she and the girls used, as he had a basement in his farmhouse that was completely empty. Finished, but unfurnished. A lot of her things would go there.

She'd been through it all before, and she drew in a deep breath, held it, and told herself to stop obsessing over it. Everything would get moved from Coral Canyon to Dog Valley, and she and Zach would decide what to do with it then.

"Morning, Mom." Ruth gave her a side-hug and reached for her coffee mug, which sat in the dish drainer. "Are you ready for today?"

"I think so," Celia said, turning to lean against the kitchen counter as her daughter doctored up her coffee. "Still no diamond on your finger?"

"No." Ruth smiled at her and threw in another spoonful of sugar. "Honestly, I thought I'd have one by now. Brandon even said he thought we should book something for that last week of April or first week of May." She shook her head. "But he hasn't asked the right question yet."

"He will," Celia said, knowing that Brandon had asked Zach for ten minutes of his time that day. Neither Celia nor Zach knew exactly why, but Celia suspected it was to talk to him about asking for Ruth's hand in marriage.

Her Brandon had done the same thing.

Ruth looked flustered and a bit embarrassed, and Celia could only wrap her arms around her daughter and tell her to hold on a few more days. She'd told herself that so many times over the years.

A few days could cure a cold, ease the worry she had for her daughters while they took their tests or applied for colleges, and the absolute desperation she felt from time to time as she'd raised her girls by herself.

She and Ruth chatted while they put together the blueberry muffins, and she'd just pulled out the first pan of muffins when Reagan showed up in the kitchen. She wore slippers and pajama pants with a tank top, and her husband followed her.

"Morning, Ma," she said with a grin. "You're getting married today." She drew Celia into a hug, and they all laughed.

"It's a little weird," Celia said. "That's for sure."

A knock sounded on the door, and she went to let in

the cowboys. "Put more muffins in, Ruthie," she said over her shoulder. On her front steps, she found her brothers.

"Heya, sis," Mack said, pulling her into a hug too. "Something smells good in here."

"We haven't even started the bacon yet." She stepped out of her brother's arms and hugged Lennox too. "Come in, the truck's not even here yet." She checked down the street after her brothers had come in, but she didn't hear or see any other pickups coming yet.

"Where are the wives?" she asked.

"O's trying to get the kids up and going," Lennox said. "She'll bring them over with Claire to clean in a couple of hours."

"The house should be fairly empty by then," Celia said, a sudden urge of sadness rolling over her. She'd experienced that a lot in the last few weeks and months as she went through everything she'd accumulated over the years.

"Come on," Lennox said. "This is a good move."

"I know," Celia said. And she did know. Another knock had her turning back to the door, but it opened before she could take a step.

Her soon-to-be-husband walked in, his face lighting up when he saw her. "Hey, gorgeous," he said, taking her into his arms and kissing her right in front of everyone. "I'm starving."

"Muffins in there," she said. "Rae's in charge of the bacon, so I think you know how that's going."

"I heard that," Reagan called from the kitchen.

"Have you talked to Brandon today?" Celia asked.

"Yeah," Zach said, his smile widening. He nodded and glanced at Ruth. "Yeah, I sure did." He started to walk away from her, and Celia just stared at his back as he shook hands with her brothers and started chatting with her daughters.

And...she supposed he wasn't going to tell her what that conversation was about. But Celia still knew.

Another batch of muffins came out, and a few pounds of bacon sat on paper towels by the time Graham and Beau showed up. Immediately following them, Andrew and Eli arrived, along with Finn, Sam Buttars, Todd and Liam, and Jack Everett. The outpouring of love and support touched Celia's heart, and she simply said, "The items tagged with the green tape stays. Everything else goes."

"You heard her," Graham said. "Everything else goes. Load 'em up, boys."

⚜

HOURS LATER, she stood in the bedroom she'd once stayed in at Zach's house, feeling absolutely beautiful in her wedding dress. No, she wasn't as skinny as she'd been the first time. She didn't have all the frills the younger girls had. But she felt like a queen, and she had the tiara to prove it.

Reagan finished tying her sash, and Ruth handed her the glittery crown. They worked together to pin it on, and then her daughters stepped back. "You're so pretty, Mom," Ruth said.

She turned away from the mirror and faced her girls—her whole world for so long. "I love you two," she said. "So much. You know that, right?"

"Of course we know that, Ma," Reagan said, swiping at her eyes. They embraced, and Reagan checked her reflection in the mirror, tucking a wayward strand of hair back where it belonged.

A soft knock sounded on the door, and Ruth stepped over to open it. "Oh." The surprise in the sound caught everyone's attention, and Celia watched as a very nervous Brandon Thompson stepped into the room.

"Hey," he said. "I know it's almost time for the wedding. I just wanted to talk to you really fast." He swallowed, and Celia reached for Ruth's hand as she nodded at Brandon.

"Ruth," he said, facing her. "I'm desperately in love with you, and I've already talked to Zach about everything. He said he'd walk you down the aisle, and he said he and Celia would love to...." He cleared his throat and glanced at Celia. "I asked for his blessing, and he gave it."

Ruth started sniffling, and Brandon dropped to both knees. He fumbled in his pocket, and he was so darn cute. "Will you marry me?" He held up a diamond ring, such bright hope in those brown eyes.

"Yes," Ruth said as she cried. Brandon swooped up and gathered her right into his arms, whispering as he kissed her.

"Yay, Ruthie!" Reagan said, engulfing everyone in a bear hug, Brandon included. Celia could barely keep her own eyes dry, and she only wished Zach could be there for this as well.

"It's time," Amanda said, poking her head into the room. "Girls, you better go sit down. Celia, your mother made it." She smiled at her friend, and Celia pulled one more time on her sleeve to make sure it lay flat.

Everyone moved out of the room, Ruth practically tripping over her heels as she admired her ring more than paying attention to where she was walking.

"Are you ready for this?" Amanda asked, stepping into the room. "Graham's as nervous as a cat in a room full of rocking chairs." She gave a light laugh. "You should see him. He's pacing and muttering to himself."

Celia laughed, though her nerves felt off the charts as well. "I'm just glad he was willing to walk this old lady down the aisle."

Amanda scoffed. "Please, you're not an old lady. Now let's go get you married." She hooked her arm through Amanda's and walked with her down the hall and into the kitchen. Graham stood there, and he turned toward them as they came closer.

He was dashing in his black suit and cowboy hat, his tie all tied up nice and neat. Amanda passed Celia to her son, and she bustled out the door with, "Give me thirty seconds, okay?"

Celia looked up at Graham. "Thank you, Graham," she said. "For everything you've done for me over the years."

"Oh, I've done nothing," he said. "You're the one who made sure us Whittakers didn't starve."

She squeezed his arm. "I love you like my own son."

He nodded, his eyes storming with emotion. "I love you like a second mom. I promise I won't let you trip down those steps."

"That would be great," she said, and she started forward with Graham. It wasn't terribly warm outside, but it wasn't cold either—the perfect weather for a wedding on a farm. The sun shone in the blue sky, and the only things that testified that it was fall were the brightly colored leaves and the chilly breeze.

Down the steps and into the backyard, which Finn had come over and helped Zach whip into perfect shape, and Celia looked down the aisle of white folding chairs to where Zach stood waiting for her.

Love shone from him like light, and the same feeling moved through Celia. She couldn't believe that just a few short months ago, she'd started thinking about dating. And then she'd met a man, and everything about him had seemed impossible.

Celia looked left and right at those she loved most, noticing that Zach's mother had come to the wedding, but his father had not. Owen and his family were there too, as well as Zach's other brothers and their families.

Forgiveness was a powerful force, and Celia was sure it would work on Zach's father's heart until he could soften up enough to let it in.

Graham kissed Celia's forehead and passed her to Zach

with the words, "You're the luckiest man alive right now," before he sat down in the front row next to his mother.

"You weren't kidding about the crown," Zach said, grinning first at it and then at her.

"I really wasn't." She faced the pastor, ready for her happily-ever-after with this handsome cowboy. Maybe it had come a little later for her than for others. Maybe she hadn't had to wait as long as she had to start dating. None of that mattered right now.

God had put Zach in her life right when she needed him, and He'd provided a way for them to be together.

His pastor gave a brief speech, and then it was time to say I do.

When it was Celia's turn, she said it loud, glad when Zach did the same. He kissed her as he laughed, and then he turned to their family and friends, who stood on their feet, clapping. He raised their joined hands, and Celia had never experienced such joy.

CHAPTER 26

Zach shrugged into his coat, which he'd just taken off an hour ago. It still felt wet, but he wouldn't dare suggest they not make the hour-long drive to Whiskey Mountain Lodge for the tree lighting ceremony.

Celia had told him a dozen times that it wasn't a ceremony. Just a family tradition, but the way she'd described what happened, it felt like a ceremony. He wanted to go, but the snow had been falling for thirty minutes, prompting them to leave earlier than they'd planned.

"You have what you need?" he asked when he met her in the garage.

"I just need to grab that box of bread. You got your bag?"

"In the back," he said, indicating the SUV they'd bought since they'd been married. She didn't like driving a truck, and he didn't want her driving her sedan up to the lodge in the winter. Not from Dog Valley.

He took the box of bread from her when she came back into the garage and put it in the back of four-by-four, next to their overnight bags. He didn't particularly want his first Christmas with Celia to be spent at Whiskey Mountain Lodge, but she'd taught him to never go to the lodge without an overnight bag.

The weather could change on a dime up there, and it was ultra-unforgiving. He'd already slept in jeans for one night, and he didn't want to repeat that, thank you very much.

With everything loaded, and both of their seatbelts buckled, he set off for the lodge. The drive wasn't bad, but it also wasn't fast, but they arrived whole and in good spirits.

The lodge itself seemed to have a personality all its own, and they were some of the first to arrive. Reagan had gone to Dale's for the holiday, and Ruth had gone to meet Brandon's parents as well, leaving Celia and Zach to come to the lodge alone.

"Celia," Stockton said, running over to her. "Dad said I could enter the bake-off at school. He said you'd help me."

"Of course I will," she said, beaming down at him. "What do you want to make?" She hugged him close to her, and Stockton grabbed onto Zach too, hugging him quickly before he returned to Celia.

Zach often felt like Celia's sidekick, but he didn't mind. She did possess a powerful charm that called people to her, especially children, and Zach liked being with her no matter what.

"I was thinking about that chocolate pie," Stockton said.

She guided him to the door and said, "Go grab something from the truck, Stocky. Let me think about the pie." She met Zach's eyes. "No way he can make that pie."

"No?"

"Maybe cookies," she mused. "You can take that bread into the kitchen."

Zach did as she said, saying hello to Beau and Lily, who sat at the breakfast bar, chatting.

Before long, the lodge filled up as more people arrived. The Christmas tree stood twenty-five feet tall in the living room, and whoever had decorated it had done a spectacular job.

Rose arrived, and Zach took a baby from her, one of the highlights of his life being joined with Celia's. He took the boy around to look at all the stockings hanging on the mantel, as well as along the walls.

He paused in front of a bright blue stocking with the baby's name on it. "Look at that, Jackson. That one's for you." And it had a gift in it. He grinned down at the little boy, and he smiled back.

Zach kept moving around the room, once again surprised when he came to stop in front of a stocking with his name on it.

His name.

Warmth filled him from head to toe, and he suddenly

understood the magic of belonging to this family. Celia had been trying to tell him for a long time. He'd been up the lodge for Sunday afternoon lunch, and he liked everyone who came. And not everyone came every week, but just as their family situations allowed.

"Oh, you found your stocking." Celia smiled at him as she slipped something inside.

"You didn't say anything about bringing gifts for the stockings," he said. "I don't have anything."

She giggled at him and waved a couple of fingers at baby Jackson. "*I* brought gifts for us, silly."

"So first we do gifts, and then we light the tree, and then we eat."

"No, we light the tree first. Gifts second." She nudged him with her elbow. "Now, can you hand out chocolate bars while holding that cute baby?"

"I think I can handle that." He took a handful of candy bars and started around the room. "Every stocking?"

"All the adults," she said. "And the bigger kids. Bailey and Stockton and Averie. Not the babies."

"Right." Zach did the task, finishing just as Graham called, "Time to begin. Everyone to the tree!"

People began pouring into the living room, taking up spots on the couches and chairs. He went over to the steps so he'd be out of the way, glad when Rose didn't take Jackson from him. In fact, Meg came over and asked, "Can you handle another one? He keeps fussing, and you're the best with him."

"Lay him on me," Zach said, taking Isaiah from her.

The boy instantly quieted, and Zach pressed a kiss to the baby's cheek. "Gotta be quiet now, bud. I think this is important."

Celia joined him on the steps, and he passed Jackson to her so he could focus on Isaiah. He'd held him while the other babies were born, and they had a special bond.

"Welcome to the lodge, everyone," Beau said, all of his brothers standing in front of the fireplace with him. "We have so many new people this year. Zach Zuckerman, of course." Beau grinned at him.

"And like, a million babies," Graham said. "Which is so great. We love babies around here." He looked down the row to Eli and Andrew. "Anyone have any announcements?"

"Why are you looking at me?" Andrew asked.

"Maybe because you guys always seem to have news," Graham said.

"Our baby is literally three months old," Andrew said.

"Eli?" Beau asked.

"Nothing for us this year," Eli said.

The brothers surveyed the group. "Anyone else?"

Amanda raised her hand, and Graham's eyebrows shot so high, several people laughed. "Mom?"

"Finn's daughter just got engaged."

"Oh, that's great," Graham said, his relief evident. "Ruth, Celia's daughter, is getting married this year as well."

"We've decided we're going to go on a church mission," Jack Everett said, looking at his wife, Fran.

"We'll leave in May for the summer, and we've signed up to go to Costa Rica."

"Really?" Lily asked at the same time as her sisters.

Once they settled down, Eli said, "Okay, should we light the tree?"

"Yep," Beau said. "Every year, we get this tree as a family. A different brother is assigned to decorate it, and this year, our beautiful tree was done by Eli's family."

"Meg did most of it," Eli said. "And Stockton." He smiled at his family.

"Averie helped on the bottom branches, didn't you, baby?" Meg smiled at her daughter.

"And every year, someone has the honor of flipping the switch and lighting the tree," Graham said. "Sometimes we know who it is, and sometimes it changes based on the announcements. But no one had anything too terribly exciting." He glanced down the row.

"Except for you thought I was pregnant," Amanda said, and everyone laughed, Zach included.

He loved the banter here. The way this family had expanded and brought in anyone who wanted to join. It wasn't just Whittakers. But Whittakers and Everetts. The men they loved, the families they had. And Celia wasn't the only one there they employed, as Zach knew Bree did a bunch of work around the lodge, as did Annie, and they were both there that night.

"Anyway," Graham said, taking his hat off and putting it back on. "This year, we thought we'd ask our second mother to light the tree."

Every eye swung toward where Celia and Zach sat on the steps together, and she pulled in a tight breath. "Really?" she asked. "Me?"

"Get up here, Celia," Beau said in his booming voice. "It's not hard."

Zach grinned as he took Jackson back, and he held a baby boy on each knee as he watched his wife pick her way through the legs and bodies to the fireplace.

His wife.

Oh, how he loved her.

"On, three...two...one...." Graham counted down, and Celia pressed the switch, lighting the tree.

Everyone ahh'ed, and Zach had to distinctly tell himself to look away from the beautiful woman he loved and look at the tree. It was glorious and beautiful, all lit up with white lights, clear to the top, where a huge star sat.

Applause began, and he couldn't join in because of the babies. But he felt the celebration down inside his soul.

And he knew Celia had been absolutely right—he never wanted to be anywhere but at Whiskey Mountain Lodge during Christmastime.

She helped pass out the stockings, and he just watched her, overcome with gratitude and love for her, for this family, for all of these people. Chatter lifted into the air as the small stocking gifts were revealed, and finally Celia said, "Come on, everyone. Time to eat."

She stood by the door and smiled at everyone as they

walked by. Zach was one of the last, and he paused right in front of her.

"This is the best Christmas I've had in a long time," he said. "Thank you."

"Next year, we can bring your kids." She grinned and took Jackson from him again.

Zach nodded, his throat tight. He couldn't wait to share this tradition with his children, who were all with their mother this year. "I love you, Celia."

"I love you too," she said. And he knew she did. She'd gone with him to take simple gifts to his brothers and his parents. No, his father hadn't come out of the bedroom, but Zach knew he eventually would. She'd put her personal touch on his house and farm in Dog Valley. And when she stretched up and kissed him, he could feel her love for him in all the right ways.

"Come on," she said. "We're waiting on you so we can eat."

"Oh, ho," he said, finally stepping into the kitchen. After all, he was hungry, and he didn't want to cause a riot among all these people.

"Right here, Zach," Stockton said as if Zach couldn't find his spot. He grinned at the boy and sat down, Celia clearly in charge of dinner.

"Merry Christmas, everyone," she said. Her voice silenced, and she looked around at everyone. "Yep. Just Merry Christmas. Let's eat."

The End

SNEAK PEEK! RHETT'S MAKE-BELIEVE MARRIAGE
CHAPTER ONE

"It's totally fine," Evelyn Foster said to the woman on the other end of the line. "Not every first date goes well." She often had to counsel her clients through a few dates before they could see what she saw.

Being a small-town matchmaker, where ninety percent of the men were cowboys, wasn't an easy job. But Evelyn loved it, as she could make everything line up on paper like a dream. The women knew what she was doing, but the men...well, sometimes men just needed to get out of their own way.

And Evelyn provided a way for them to do that—and conveniently run into the woman of their dreams. They just didn't know it yet.

And obviously, Tina didn't know it yet either. "He's perfect for you," Evelyn assured her. "What happened that rubbed you the wrong way?"

"For starters, he wanted to take me to the big box store

for a date."

Evelyn could hear the eyeroll in Tina's voice.

"But you persuaded him to do something else, right?" Evelyn asked, shuffling a couple of pages on the desk in front of her. The wind shook the windows of her office, and she glanced outside to see a dust storm had kicked up on the farm where she lived with her sisters.

Granted, they didn't really use the two hundred acres they had, as that was a lot for three women to manage by themselves. Their father had retired a few years ago, and they mostly planted as much as they could and sold the hay to other farms and ranches surrounding Three Rivers.

"I did, yes," Tina said. "But is that going to be my whole life moving forward? Me trying to persuade this guy to do what I want?"

"Let me look through a few more candidates," Evelyn said, focusing on her papers again. May was an exceptionally busy time for her services, as well as around Shining Star Ranch. While her oldest sister, Callie, ran most of what happened on the ranch, Evelyn had plenty of chores to do too. "And I'll get back to you in a couple of days, okay?"

"Okay," Tina said. "What should I do if Gideon calls?"

"You get to decide that," Evelyn said, looking at Gideon's one-sheet. "He really does seem perfect for you. Maybe he just didn't want to commit to something as long as dinner."

"I don't know how that's a plus," Tina said dryly.

"Well, he's met you once, for what? Five minutes at

the dry cleaner? Somewhere I only knew he'd be because we got a last-minute phone call." Evelyn never revealed her sources, but she had spies all over the town of Three Rivers.

With a population of almost seventeen thousand now, she certainly couldn't be everywhere at once, or know where every eligible bachelor would be at any given time.

"And that was the first time he'd been there," Evelyn reminded her. "So maybe give him a little slack?" She spoke as kindly as she could. After all, Tina was paying her, and she didn't need to lose a client because the cowboy Tina had her eye on was out of his element.

"Okay." Tina sighed. "But still look at a couple of other guys for me."

"Anyone in mind?" Evelyn asked, because no one else on her list stood out for someone like Tina. She liked a through-and-through Texas cowboy, with a big hat, and the biggest belt buckle possible. Rodeo experience a plus.

While there were plenty of cowboys in Three Rivers, Tina wanted Cowboy Extreme.

"I've seen a man at church the last few weeks," Tina said. "He looks new in town."

Evelyn repressed a sigh and looked out the window again. She couldn't see the trees she knew were only ten feet away. Alarms started sounding in her mind, and surprise darted through her that she hadn't lost cell phone reception yet.

"I don't know his name or where he lives," Tina said.

"All right," Evelyn said. "I'll put out some feelers to

find out who this guy is." With that, the line crackled, and Tina's words broke up. In the next moment, the service cut out, and Evelyn looked at her phone to see the call had indeed been severed.

"Great," she muttered. Now she had to hunt down a mystery cowboy who was new to town. Maybe Patrick would know. Her boyfriend worked the meat counter at the grocery store, and he saw a lot of people—especially single cowboys coming to buy their steak dinners.

Of course, a lot of the cowboys around Three Rivers worked on farms and ranches, and they often got plenty of beef for free from their employers. So maybe Patrick wouldn't know. But it couldn't hurt to ask him.

He knew what Evelyn did for a living, and he often sent her texts with information on men she needed to know about. She couldn't send him a text right then, as it seemed her provider had gone down with the crazy windstorm.

She left her office at the same time a horrible, glass-shattering sound filled the whole farmhouse. She screamed, hers matching her younger sister's in the living room.

Callie burst in the back door with the words, "There's a tornado headed this way. Come help me with the animals." She spun away before either Evelyn or Simone could answer.

Thankfully, Evelyn already had shoes on, and she hurried after her oldest sister, saying, "The sirens haven't even gone off. Maybe it's just a windstorm."

The moment she finished speaking, the chilling, distinct wail of the tornado siren filled the air.

She ran after Callie, who handed her a grease pen and a handful of fly masks. "Put our phone number on their sides. Put on the fly mask, and we'll set them in the pasture."

They didn't have the hurricane clips or reinforced beams needed to tether the horses securely in the barn, and their horses were used to roaming in pastures.

"Maybe it'll go north," Callie said, her voice panicked. "Like that last one."

The last tornado had been over two years ago, and it had indeed turned north before inflicting too much damage on Three Rivers. She handed Simone the same items she had Evelyn, and the sisters got to work.

"We have to go next door, too," Callie said. "We'll put our number on the animals at Fox Hill for the new owner."

"Who is it?" Evelyn asked, glancing east though she couldn't see more than five feet in either direction. Even Callie's voice coming through the swirling dirt and dust felt eerie and otherworldly.

"Some guy," Callie said vaguely, which meant she didn't know either. "Last name's Walker, I think. Mason texted a couple of days ago and said he'd be here this week, and that we could turn the keys over to him then."

Mason Martin had lived and cultivated Fox Hill Ranch next door for years and years before deciding to up and move to Hawaii, of all places. He'd put the ranch up for sale, and contracted with the sisters to take care of the few animals he'd left behind. He had a staff of four still on the premises too, and Evelyn wondered why they couldn't take care of their own horses.

"What about Orion?" she asked. "Can't he turn the horses out to pasture over there?" It was at least a half-mile to Fox Hill, though their properties touched one another along a fence line on the east side of the ranch. Evelyn did *not* want to get caught out in the storm.

"They went into town this morning," Callie said, finishing with her last horse, smacking it on the flank and saying, "Go on. Stay safe."

With their own livestock numbered and protected as much as possible, the three sisters piled into Callie's pickup truck and rumbled down the road. If anything, the wind blew stronger at Fox Hill, but Evelyn kept her head down and her fingers moving as she marked the eight horses Mason had left behind.

He also had two pigs, six goats, and a whole herd of chickens. The tornado would likely pick them up and carry them off, and she certainly didn't know how to hold one long enough to write a phone number on feathers.

With all the animals marked that could be, Callie shouted, "We have to go inside!"

Exactly what Evelyn didn't want to do, at least not here. But one look at the sky, and she knew she didn't have a choice. Panic filled her, though she'd lived through tornadoes before. They weren't super common in this area of Texas, but she'd had enough experience with them to know what to do in case of an emergency.

"Where's Daddy?" Simone asked.

"He's with Granny," Callie yelled, holding her hat on her head as she ran for the back door of Mason's homestead.

It felt strangely quiet inside, with the three of them panting as they sucked at air that finally wasn't filled with debris.

"Come on," Callie said. "He'll have a tornado shelter."

Evelyn had been to Mason's house several times, and she knew right where it was. As Callie turned to go down a hallway, she said, "It's over here, guys. He showed it to me once." She hated that she wasn't in her own home, protecting it and herself.

But just inside the living room off the front door, she swept aside the rug and pointed to the hatch door there. "Goes down into a cement foundation."

"Get in," Callie said as glass broke somewhere in the house. The tornado might not strike Three Rivers directly, but this wind was definitely wicked and causing some real damage.

Evelyn went first and turned on her phone's flashlight. Callie followed and did the same, with Simone bringing up the rear. No sooner had Simone closed the door above them and come down the steps did it open again.

Callie shone her flashlight on the man sliding down the steps, pure fear in every line on his face. "Who are you?" she asked as Evelyn swung her light onto him too.

He bore a strong jaw and dark eyes—exactly the kind of man Evelyn would be interested in. You know, if she wasn't already dating someone.

The stranger drew in a deep breath and spoke in an even deeper voice. "I'm Rhett Walker. This is my ranch." He dusted himself off with a pair of big hands and added, "You must be the Foster sisters from next door."

"Guilty," Callie said, lowering her light so it wasn't shining right in Rhett's face. But Evelyn couldn't do the same. His good looks and bass voice seemed to have frozen her to the spot, and all she could do was stare while her heart pounded wildly in her chest.

"Can you stop shining that in my face?" he asked, his voice a touch colder than before, and Callie put her hand on Evelyn's arm to make her put the phone down.

"So," he said with only the soft glow on his features now. He was somehow sexier and more beautiful than in the harsh light, and Evelyn wondered where in the world all these thoughts and feelings were coming from. "I guess the tornado is welcoming me to the Texas Panhandle." He laughed, and Simone and Callie joined him.

Evelyn simply reveled in the sound of his laughter, thinking that if she weren't with Patrick, she'd definitely be setting herself up with one cowboy Rhett Walker.

Callie started to detail what they'd done for his animals and why they'd come in his house instead of theirs, and Evelyn shied behind her sister so she could continue to simply stare at her new next-door neighbor.

BOOKS IN THE CHRISTMAS IN CORAL CANYON ROMANCE SERIES

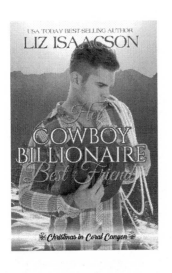

Her Cowboy Billionaire Best Friend (Book 1): Graham Whittaker returns to Coral Canyon a few days after Christmas—after the death of his father. He takes over the energy company his dad built from the ground up and buys a high-end lodge to live in—only a mile from the home of his once-best friend, Laney McAllister. They were best friends once, but Laney's always entertained feelings for him, and spending so much time with him while they make Christmas memories puts her heart in danger of getting broken again...

Her Cowboy Billionaire Boss (Book 2): Since the death of his wife a few years ago, Eli Whittaker has been running from one job to another, unable to find somewhere for him and his son to settle. Meg Palmer is Stockton's nanny, and she comes with her boss, Eli, to the lodge, her long-time crush on the man no different in Wyoming than it was on the beach. When she confesses her feelings for him and gets nothing in return, she's crushed, embarrassed, and unsure if she can stay in Coral Canyon for Christmas. Then Eli starts to show some feelings for her too...

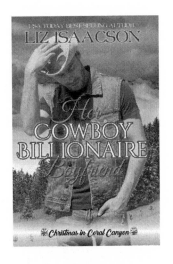

Her Cowboy Billionaire Boyfriend (Book 3): Andrew Whittaker is the public face for the Whittaker Brothers' family energy company, and with his older brother's robot about to be announced, he needs a press secretary to help him get everything ready and tour the state to make the announcements. When he's hit by a protest sign being carried by the company's biggest opponent, Rebecca Collings, he learns with a few clicks that she has the background they need. He offers her the job of press secretary when she thought she was going to be arrested, and not only because the spark between them in so hot Andrew can't see straight.

Can Becca and Andrew work together and keep their relationship a secret? Or will hearts break in this classic romance retelling reminiscent of *Two Weeks Notice*?

Her Cowboy Billionaire Bodyguard (Book 4): Beau Whittaker has watched his brothers find love one by one, but every attempt he's made has ended in disaster. Lily Everett has been in the spotlight since childhood and has half a dozen platinum records with her two sisters. She's taking a break from the brutal music industry and hiding out in Wyoming while her ex-husband continues to cause trouble for her. When she hears of Beau Whittaker and what he offers his clients, she wants to meet him. Beau is instantly attracted to Lily, but he tried a relationship with his last client that left a scar that still hasn't healed...

Can Lily use the spirit of Christmas to discover what matters most? Will Beau open his heart to the possibility of love with someone so different from him?

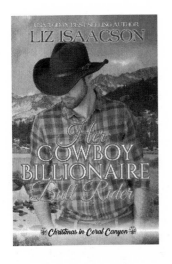

Her Cowboy Billionaire Bull Rider (Book 5): Todd Christopherson has just retired from the professional rodeo circuit and returned to his hometown of Coral Canyon. Problem is, he's got no family there anymore, no land, and no job. Not that he needs a job--he's got plenty of money from his illustrious career riding bulls.

Then Todd gets thrown during a routine horseback ride up the canyon, and his only support as he recovers physically is the beautiful Violet Everett. She's no nurse, but she does the best she can for the handsome cowboy. **Will she lose her heart to the billionaire bull rider? Can Todd trust that God led him to Coral Canyon...and Vi?**

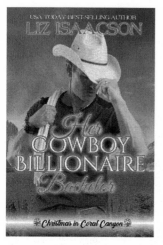

Her Cowboy Billionaire Bachelor (Book 6): Rose Everett isn't sure what to do with her life now that her country music career is on hold. After all, with both of her sisters in Coral Canyon, and one about to have a baby, they're not making albums anymore.

Liam Murphy has been working for Doctors Without Borders, but he's back in the US now, and looking to start a new clinic in Coral Canyon, where he spent his summers.

When Rose wins a date with Liam in a bachelor auction, their relationship blooms and grows quickly. **Can Liam and Rose find a solution to their problems that doesn't involve one of them leaving Coral Canyon with a broken heart?**

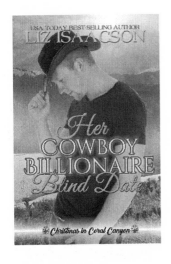

Christmas in Coral Canyon

Her Cowboy Billionaire Blind Date (Book 7): Her sons want her to be happy, but she's too old to be set up on a blind date...isn't she?

Amanda Whittaker has been looking for a second chance at love since the death of her husband several years ago. Finley Barber is a cowboy in every sense of the word. Born and raised on a racehorse farm in Kentucky, he's since moved to Dog Valley and started his own breeding stable for champion horses. He hasn't dated in years, and everything about Amanda makes him nervous.

Will Amanda take the leap of faith required to be with Finn? Or will he become just another boyfriend who doesn't make the cut?

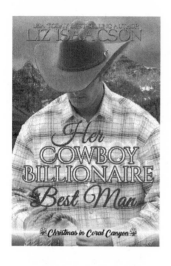

Her Cowboy Billionaire Best Man (Book 8): When Celia Abbott-Armstrong runs into a gorgeous cowboy at her best friend's wedding, she decides she's ready to start dating again.

But the cowboy is Zach Zuckerman, and the Zuckermans and Abbotts have been at war for generations.

Can Zach and Celia find a way to reconcile their family's differences so they can have a future together?

BOOKS IN THE SEVEN SONS RANCH IN
THREE RIVERS ROMANCE SERIES

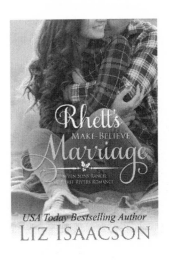

Rhett's Make-Believe Marriage (Book 1): She needs a husband to be credible as a matchmaker. He wants to help a neighbor. Will their fake marriage take them out of the friend zone?

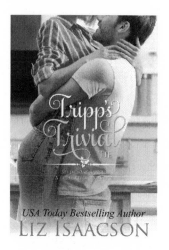

USA Today Bestselling Author
LIZ ISAACSON

Tripp's Trivial Tie (Book 2):
She needs a husband to keep her son. He's wanted to take their relationship to the next level, but she's always pushing him away. Will their trivial tie take them all the way to happily-ever-after?

Liam's Invented I-Do (Book 3): She needs a husband to be credible as a matchmaker. He wants to help a neighbor. Will their fake marriage take them out of the friend zone?

BOOKS IN THE LAST CHANCE RANCH ROMANCE SERIES

Her Last First Kiss (Book 1): A cowgirl down on her luck hires a man who's good with horses and under the hood of a car. Can Hudson fine tune Scarlett's heart as they work together? Or will things backfire and make everything worse at Last Chance Ranch?

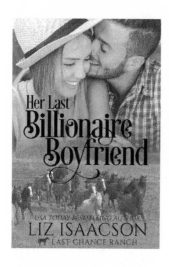

Her Last Billionaire Boyfriend (Book 2): A billionaire cowboy without a home meets a woman who secretly makes food videos to pay her debts...Can Carson and Adele do more than fight in the kitchens at Last Chance Ranch?

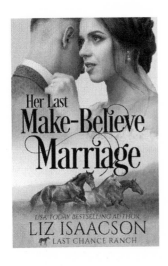

Her Last Make-Believe Marriage (Book 3): A female carpenter needs a husband just for a few days... Can Jeri and Sawyer navigate the minefield of a pretend marriage before their feelings become real?

Her Last Second Chance (Book 4): An Army cowboy, the woman he dated years ago, and their last chance at Last Chance Ranch... Can Dave and Sissy put aside hurt feelings and make their second chance romance work?

Her Last Secret Sweetheart (Book 5): A former dairy farmer and the marketing director on the ranch have to work together to make the cow cuddling program a success. But can Karla let Cache into her life? Or will she keep all her secrets from him - and keep *him* a secret too?

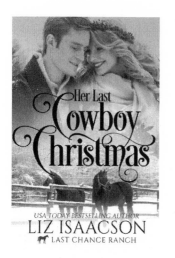

USA TODAY BESTSELLING AUTHOR
LIZ ISAACSON
LAST CHANCE RANCH

Her Last Cowboy Christmas (Book 6): She's tired of having her heart broken by cowboys. He waited too long to ask her out. Can Lance fix things quickly, or will Amber leave Last Chance Ranch before he can tell her how he feels?

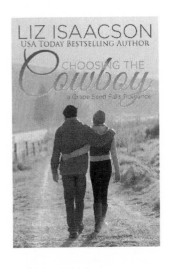

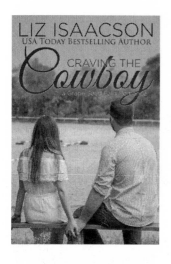

Craving the Cowboy (Book 2): Dwayne Carver is set to inherit his family's ranch in the heart of Texas Hill Country, and in order to keep up with his ranch duties and fulfill his dreams of owning a horse farm, he hires top trainer Felicity Lightburne. They get along great, and she can envision herself on this new farm—at least until her mother falls ill and she has to return to help her. Can Dwayne and Felicity work through their differences to find their happily-ever-after?

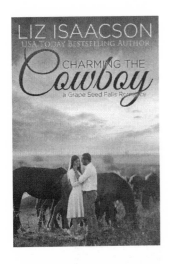

Charming the Cowboy (Book 3): Third grade teacher Heather Carver has had her eye on Levi Rhodes for a couple of years now, but he seems to be blind to her attempts to charm him. When she breaks her arm while on his horse ranch, Heather infiltrates Levi's life in ways he's never thought of, and his strict anti-female stance slips. Will Heather heal his emotional scars and he care for her physical ones so they can have a real relationship?

Courting the Cowboy (Book 4): Frustrated with the cowboy-only dating scene in Grape Seed Falls, May Sotheby joins TexasFaithful.com, hoping to find her soul mate without having to relocate--or deal with cowboy hats and boots. She has no idea that Kurt Pemberton, foreman at Grape Seed Ranch, is the man she starts communicating with... Will May be able to follow her heart and get Kurt to forgive her so they can be together?

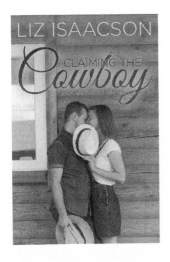

Claiming the Cowboy, Royal Brothers Book 1 (Grape Seed Falls Romance Book 5): Unwilling to be tied down, farrier Robin Cook has managed to pack her entire life into a two-hundred-and-eighty square-foot house, and that includes her Yorkie. Cowboy and co-foreman, Shane Royal has had his heart set on Robin for three years, even though she flat-out turned him down the last time he asked her to dinner. But she's back at Grape Seed Ranch for five weeks as she works her horse-shoeing magic, and he's still interested, despite a bitter life lesson that left a bad taste for marriage in his mouth.

Robin's interested in him too. But can she find room for Shane in her tiny house--and can he take a chance on her with his tired heart?

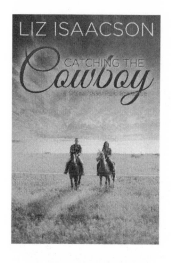

Catching the Cowboy, Royal Brothers Book 2 (Grape Seed Falls Romance Book 6): Dylan Royal is good at two things: whistling and caring for cattle. When his cows are being attacked by an unknown wild animal, he calls Texas Parks & Wildlife for help. He wasn't expecting a beautiful mammologist to show up, all flirty and fun and everything Dylan didn't know he wanted in his life.

Hazel Brewster has gone on more first dates than anyone in Grape Seed Falls, and she thinks maybe Dylan deserves a second... Can they find their way through wild animals, huge life changes, and their emotional pasts to find their forever future?

Cheering the Cowboy, Royal Brothers Book 3 (Grape Seed Falls Romance Book 7): Austin Royal loves his life on his new ranch with his brothers. But he doesn't love that Shayleigh Hatch came with the property, nor that he has to take the blame for the fact that he now owns her childhood ranch. They rarely have a conversation that doesn't leave him furious and frustrated--and yet he's still attracted to Shay in a strange, new way.

Shay inexplicably likes him too, which utterly confuses and angers her. As they work to make this Christmas the best the Triple Towers Ranch has ever seen, can they also navigate through their rocky relationship to smoother waters?

BOOKS IN THE STEEPLE RIDGE ROMANCE SERIES:

Her Billionaire Cowboy (Book 1): Tucker Jenkins has had enough of tall buildings, traffic, and has traded in his technology firm in New York City for Steeple Ridge Horse Farm in rural Vermont. Missy Marino has worked at the farm since she was a teen, and she's always dreamed of owning it. But her ex-husband left her with a truckload of debt, making her fantasies of owning the farm unfulfilled. Tucker didn't come to the country to find a new wife, but he supposes a woman could help him start over in Steeple Ridge. Will Tucker and Missy be able to navigate the shaky ground between them to find a new beginning?

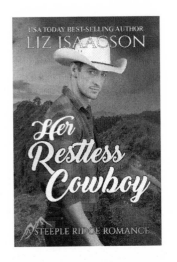

Her Restless Cowboy (Book 2): Ben Buttars is the youngest of the four Buttars brothers who come to Steeple Ridge Farm, and he finally feels like he's landed somewhere he can make a life for himself. Reagan Cantwell is a decade older than Ben and the recreational direction for the town of Island Park. Though Ben is young, he knows what he wants—and that's Rae. Can she figure out how to put what matters most in her life—family and faith—above her job before she loses Ben?

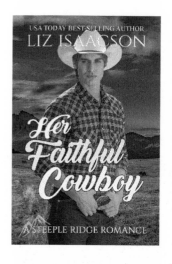

Her Faithful Cowboy (Book 3): Sam Buttars has spent the last decade making sure he and his brothers stay together. They've been at Steeple Ridge for a while now, but with the youngest married and happy, the siren's call to return to his parents' farm in Wyoming is loud in Sam's ears. He'd just go if it weren't for beautiful Bonnie Sherman, who roped his heart the first time he saw her. Do Sam and Bonnie have the faith to find comfort in each other instead of in the people who've already passed?

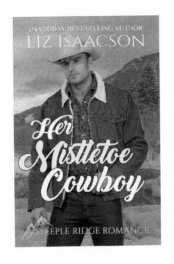

Her Mistletoe Cowboy (Book 4): Logan Buttars has always been good-natured and happy-go-lucky. After watching two of his brothers settle down, he recognizes a void in his life he didn't know about. Veterinarian Layla Guyman has appreciated Logan's friendship and easy way with animals when he comes into the clinic to get the service dogs. But with his future at Steeple Ridge in the balance, she's not sure a relationship with him is worth the risk. Can she rely on her faith and employ patience to tame Logan's wild heart?

Her Patient Cowboy (Book 5): Darren Buttars is cool, collected, and quiet—and utterly devastated when his girlfriend of nine months, Farrah Irvine, breaks up with him because he wanted her to ride her horse in a parade. But Farrah doesn't ride anymore, a fact she made very clear to Darren. She returned to her childhood home with so much baggage, she doesn't know where to start with the unpacking. Darren's the only Buttars brother who isn't married, and he wants to make Island Park his permanent home—with Farrah. Can they find their way through the heartache to achieve a happily-ever-after together?

Falling for Her Boss: A Horseshoe Home Ranch Romance (Book 1): Jace Lovell only has one thing left after his fiancé abandons him at the altar: his job at Horseshoe Home Ranch. Belle Edmunds is back in Gold Valley and she's desperate to build a portfolio that she can use to start her own firm in Montana. Jace isn't anywhere near forgiving his fiancé, and he's not sure he's ready for a new relationship with someone as fiery and beautiful as Belle. Can she employ her patience while he figures out how to forgive so they can find their own brand of happily-ever-after?

Falling for Her Roommate: A Horseshoe Home Ranch Romance (Book 2): Professional snowboarder Sterling Maughan has sequestered himself in his family's cabin in the exclusive mountain community above Gold Valley, Montana after a devastating fall that ended his career. Norah Watson cleans Sterling's cabin and the more time they spend together, the more Sterling is interested in all things Norah. As his body heals, so does his faith. Will Norah be able to trust Sterling so they can have a chance at true love?

Falling for His Best Friend: A Horseshoe Home Ranch Romance (Book 3): Landon Edmunds has been a cowboy his whole life. An accident five years ago ended his successful rodeo career, and now he's looking to start a horse ranch-- and he's looking outside of Montana. Which would be great if God hadn't brought Megan Palmer back to Gold Valley right when Landon is looking to leave. Megan and Landon work together well, and as sparks fly, she's sure God brought her back to Gold Valley so she could find her happily ever after. Through serious discussion and prayer, can Landon and Megan find their future together?

Be sure to check out the spinoff series, the Brush Creek Brides romances after you read FALLING FOR HIS BEST FRIEND. Start with A WEDDING FOR THE WIDOWER.

Falling for His Nanny: A Horseshoe Home Ranch Romance (Book 4): Twelve years ago, Owen Carr left Gold Valley—and his long-time girlfriend—in favor of a country music career in Nashville. Married and divorced, Natalie teaches ballet at the dance studio in Gold Valley, but she never auditioned for the professional company the way she dreamed of doing. With Owen back, she realizes all the opportunities she missed out on when he left all those years ago—including a future with him. Can they mend broken bridges in order to have a second chance at love?

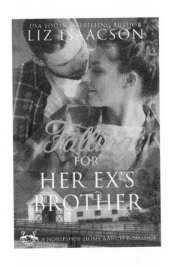

Falling for Her Ex's Brother: A Horseshoe Home Ranch Romance (Book 5): Caleb Chamberlain has spent the last five years recovering from a horrible breakup, his alcoholism that stemmed from it, and the car accident that left him hospitalized. He's finally on the right track in his life—until Holly Gray, his twin brother's ex-fiance mistakes him for Nathan. Holly's back in Gold Valley to get the required veterinarian hours to apply for her graduate program. When the herd at Horseshoe Home comes down with pneumonia, Caleb and Holly are forced to work together in close quarters. Holly's over Nathan, but she hasn't forgiven him—or the woman she believes broke up their relationship. Can Caleb and Holly navigate such a rough past to find their happily-ever-after?

Journey to Steeple Ridge Farm with Holly—and fall in love with the cowboys there in the Steeple Ridge Romance series! Start with STARTING OVER AT STEEPLE RIDGE.

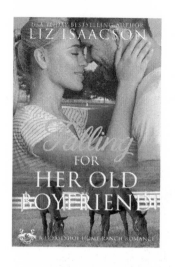

Falling for Her Old Boyfriend: A Horseshoe Home Ranch Romance (Book 6): Ty Barker has been dancing through the last thirty years of his life--and he's suddenly realized he's alone. River Lee Whitely is back in Gold Valley with her two little girls after a divorce that's left deep scars. She has a job at Silver Creek that requires her to be able to ride a horse, and she nearly tramples Ty at her first lesson. That's just fine by him, because River Lee is the girl Ty has never gotten over. Ty realizes River Lee needs time to settle into her new job, her new home, her new life as a single parent, but going slow has never been his style. But for River Lee, can Ty take the necessary steps to keep her in his life?

Falling for His Next Door Neighbor: A Horseshoe Home Ranch Romance (Book 7): Archer Bailey has already lost one job to Emersyn Enders, so he deliberately doesn't tell her about the cowhand job up at Horseshoe Home Ranch. Emery's temporary job is ending, but her obligations to her physically disabled sister aren't. As Archer and Emery work together, its clear that the sparks flying between them aren't all from their friendly competition over a job. Will Emery and Archer be able to navigate the ranch, their close quarters, and their individual circumstances to find love this holiday season?

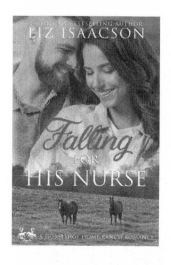

Falling for His Nurse: A Horseshoe Home Ranch Romance (Book 8): Cowboy Elliott Hawthorne has just lost his best friend and cabin mate to the worst thing imaginable —marriage. When his brother calls about an accident with their father, Elliott rushes down to Gold Valley from the ranch only to be met with the most beautiful woman he's ever seen. His father's new physical therapist, London Marsh, likes the handsome face and gentle spirit she sees in Elliott too. Can Elliott and London navigate difficult family situations to find a happily-ever-after?

Second Chance Ranch: A Three Rivers Ranch Romance (Book 1): After his deployment, injured and discharged Major Squire Ackerman returns to Three Rivers Ranch, wanting to forgive Kelly for ignoring him a decade ago. He'd like to provide the stable life she needs, but with old wounds opening and a ranch on the brink of financial collapse, it will take patience and faith to make their second chance possible.

Third Time's the Charm: A Three Rivers Ranch Romance (Book 2): First Lieutenant Peter Marshall has a truckload of debt and no way to provide for a family, but Chelsea helps him see past all the obstacles, all the scars. With so many unknowns, can Pete and Chelsea develop the love, acceptance, and faith needed to find their happily ever after?

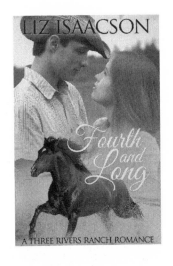

Fourth and Long: A Three Rivers Ranch Romance (Book 3): Commander Brett Murphy goes to Three Rivers Ranch to find some rest and relaxation with his Army buddies. Having his ex-wife show up with a seven-year-old she claims is his son is anything but the R&R he craves. Kate needs to make amends, and Brett needs to find forgiveness, but are they too late to find their happily ever after?

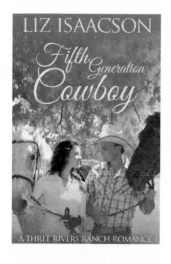

Fifth Generation Cowboy: A Three Rivers Ranch Romance (Book 4): Tom Lovell has watched his friends find their true happiness on Three Rivers Ranch, but everywhere he looks, he only sees friends. Rose Reyes has been bringing her daughter out to the ranch for equine therapy for months, but it doesn't seem to be working. Her challenges with Mari are just as frustrating as ever. Could Tom be exactly what Rose needs? Can he remove his friendship blinders and find love with someone who's been right in front of him all this time?

LIZ ISAACSON

A THREE RIVERS RANCH ROMANCE NOVELLA

Sixth Street Love Affair: A Three Rivers Ranch Romance (Book 5): After losing his wife a few years back, Garth Ahlstrom thinks he's ready for a second chance at love. But Juliette Thompson has a secret that could destroy their budding relationship. Can they find the strength, patience, and faith to make things work?

A THREE RIVERS RANCH ROMANCE

The Seventh Sergeant: A Three Rivers Ranch Romance (Book 6): Life has finally started to settle down for Sergeant Reese Sanders after his devastating injury overseas. Discharged from the Army and now with a good job at Courage Reins, he's finally found happiness—until a horrific fall puts him right back where he was years ago: Injured and depressed. Carly Watters, Reese's new veteran care coordinator, dislikes small towns almost as much as she loathes cowboys. But she finds herself faced with both when she gets assigned to Reese's case. Do they have the humility and faith to make their relationship more than professional?

Eight Second Ride: A Three Rivers Ranch Romance (Book 7): Ethan Greene loves his work at Three Rivers Ranch, but he can't seem to find the right woman to settle down with. When sassy yet vulnerable Brynn Bowman shows up at the ranch to recruit him back to the rodeo circuit, he takes a different approach with the barrel racing champion. His patience and newfound faith pay off when a friendship--and more-- starts with Brynn. But she wants out of the rodeo circuit right when Ethan wants to rejoin. Can they find the path God wants them to take and still stay together?

The First Lady of Three Rivers Ranch: A Three Rivers Ranch Romance (Book 8): Heidi Duffin has been dreaming about opening her own bakery since she was thirteen years old. She scrimped and saved for years to afford baking and pastry school in San Francisco. And now she only has one year left before she's a certified pastry chef. Frank Ackerman's father has recently retired, and he's taken over the largest cattle ranch in the Texas Panhandle. A horseman through and through, he's also nearing thirty-one and looking for someone to bring love and joy to a homestead that's been dominated by men for a decade. But when he convinces Heidi to come clean the cowboy cabins, she changes all that. But the siren's call of a bakery is still loud in Heidi's ears, even if she's also seeing a future with Frank. Can she rely on her faith in ways she's never had to before or will their relationship end when summer does?

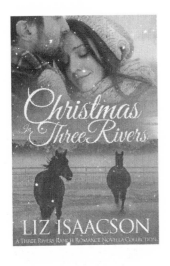

Christmas in Three Rivers: A Three Rivers Ranch Romance (Book 9): Isn't Christmas the best time to fall in love? The cowboys of Three Rivers Ranch think so. Join four of them as they journey toward their path to happily ever after in four, all-new novellas in the Amazon #1 Bestselling Three Rivers Ranch Romance series.

THE NINTH INNING: The Christmas season has never felt like such a burden to boutique owner Andrea Larsen. But with Mama gone and the holidays upon her, Andy finds herself wishing she hadn't been so quick to judge her former boyfriend, cowboy Lawrence Collins. Well, Lawrence hasn't forgotten about Andy either, and he devises a plan to get her out to the ranch so they can reconnect. Do they have the faith and humility to patch things up and start a new relationship?

TEN DAYS IN TOWN: Sandy Keller is tired of the dating scene in Three Rivers. Though she owns the pancake house, she's looking for a fresh start, which means an escape from the town where she grew up. When her older brother's best friend, Tad Jorgensen, comes to town for the holidays, it is a balm to his weary soul. A helicopter tour guide who experienced a near-death experience, he's looking to start over too--but in Three Rivers. Can Sandy and Tad navigate their troubles to find the path God wants them to take--and discover true love--in only ten days?

ELEVEN YEAR REUNION: Pastry chef extraordinaire, Grace Lewis has moved to Three Rivers to help Heidi Ackerman open a bakery in Three Rivers. Grace relishes the idea of starting over in a town where no one knows about her failed cupcakery. She doesn't expect to run into her old high school boyfriend, Jonathan Carver. A carpenter working at Three Rivers Ranch, Jon's in town against his will. But with Grace now on the scene, Jon's thinking life in Three Rivers is suddenly looking up. But with her focus on baking and his disdain for small towns, can they make their eleven year reunion stick?

THE TWELFTH TOWN: Newscaster Taryn Tucker has had enough of life on-screen. She's bounced from town to town before arriving in Three Rivers, completely alone and completely anonymous--just the way she now likes it. She takes a job cleaning at Three Rivers Ranch, hoping for a chance to figure out who she is and where God wants her. When she meets happy-go-lucky cowhand Kenny Stockton, she doesn't expect sparks to fly. Kenny's always been "the best friend" for his female friends, but the pull between him and Taryn can't be denied. Will they have the courage and faith necessary to make their opposite worlds mesh?

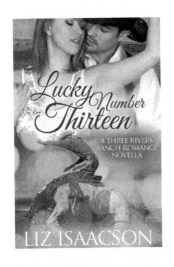

Lucky Number Thirteen: A Three Rivers Ranch Romance (Book 10): Tanner Wolf, a rodeo champion ten times over, is excited to be riding in Three Rivers for the first time since he left his philandering ways and found religion. Seeing his old friends Ethan and Brynn is therapuetic--until a terrible accident lands him in the hospital. With his rodeo career over, Tanner thinks maybe he'll stay in town--and it's not just because his nurse, Summer Hamblin, is the prettiest woman he's ever met. But Summer's the queen of first dates, and as she looks for a way to make a relationship with the transient rodeo star work Summer's not sure she has the fortitude to go on a second date. Can they find love among the tragedy?

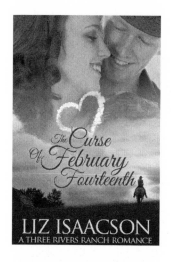

The Curse of February Fourteenth: A Three Rivers Ranch Romance (Book 11): Cal Hodgkins, cowboy veterinarian at Bowman's Breeds, isn't planning to meet anyone at the masked dance in small-town Three Rivers. He just wants to get his bachelor friends off his back and sit on the sidelines to drink his punch. But when he sees a woman dressed in gorgeous butterfly wings and cowgirl boots with blue stitching, he's smitten. Too bad she runs away from the dance before he can get her name, leaving only her boot behind...

Fifteen Minutes of Fame: A Three Rivers Ranch Romance (Book 12): Navy Richards is thirty-five years of tired—tired of dating the same men, working a demanding job, and getting her heart broken over and over again. Her aunt has always spoken highly of the matchmaker in Three Rivers, Texas, so she takes a six-month sabbatical from her high-stress job as a pediatric nurse, hops on a bus, and meets with the matchmaker. Then she meets Gavin Redd. He's handsome, he's hardworking, and he's a cowboy. But is he an Aquarius too? Navy's not making a move until she knows for sure...

Sixteen Steps to Fall in Love: A Three Rivers Ranch Romance (Book 13): A chance encounter at a dog park sheds new light on the tall, talented Boone that Nicole can't ignore. As they get to know each other better and start to dig into each other's past, Nicole is the one who wants to run. This time from her growing admiration and attachment to Boone. From her aging parents. From herself.

But Boone feels the attraction between them too, and he decides he's tired of running and ready to make Three Rivers his permanent home. **Can Boone and Nicole use their faith to overcome their differences and find a happily-ever-after together?**

The Sleigh on Seventeenth Street: A Three Rivers Ranch Romance (Book 14): A cowboy with skills as an electrician tries a relationship with a down-on-her luck plumber. Can Dylan and Camila make water and electricity play nicely together this Christmas season? Or will they get shocked as they try to make their relationship work?

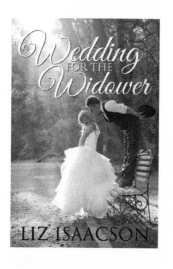

A Companion for the Cowboy: Brush Creek Brides Romance (Book 2): Cowboy and professional roper Justin Jackman has found solitude at Brush Creek Horse Ranch, preferring his time with the animals he trains over dating. With two failed engagements in his past, he's not really interested in getting his heart

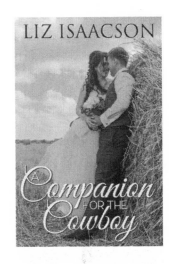

stomped on again. But when flirty and fun Renee Martin picks him up at a church ice cream bar--on a bet, no less-- he finds himself more than just a little interested. His Gen-X attitudes are attractive to her; her Millennial behaviors drive him nuts. Can Justin look past their differences and take a chance on another engagement?

A Bride for the Bronc Rider: Brush Creek Brides Romance (Book 3): Ted Caldwell has been a retired bronc rider for years, and he thought he was perfectly happy training horses to buck at Brush Creek Ranch. He was wrong. When he meets April Nox, who comes to the ranch to hide her pregnancy from all her friends back in Jackson Hole, Ted realizes he has a huge family-shaped hole in his life. April is embarrassed, heartbroken, and trying to find her extinguished faith. She's never ridden a horse and wants nothing to do with a cowboy ever again. Can Ted and April create a family of happiness and love from a tragedy?

A Family for the Farmer:
Brush Creek Brides Romance
(Book 4): Blake Gibbons over-
sees all the agriculture at Brush
Creek Horse Ranch, sometimes
moonlighting as a general
contractor. When he meets
Erin Shields, new in town, at
her aunt's bakery, he's instantly
smitten. Erin moved to Brush
Creek after a divorce that left

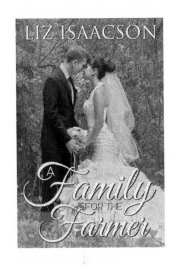

her penniless, homeless, and a single mother of three children under age eight. She's nowhere near ready to start
dating again, but the longer Blake hangs around the
bakery, the more she starts to like him. Can Blake and Erin
find a way to blend their lifestyles and become a family?

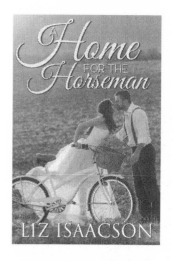

A Home for the Horseman: Brush Creek Brides Romance (Book 5): Emmett Graves has always had a positive outlook on life. He adores training horses to become barrel racing champions during the day and cuddling with his cat at night. Fresh off her professional rodeo retirement, Molly Brady comes to Brush Creek Horse Ranch as Emmett's protege. He's not thrilled, and she's allergic to cats. Oh, and she'd like to stay cowboy-free, thank you very much. But Emmett's about as cowboy as they come.... Can Emmett and Molly work together without falling in love?

A Refuge for the Rancher: Brush Creek Brides Romance (Book 6): Grant Ford spends his days training cattle—when he's not camped out at the elementary school hoping to catch a glimpse of his ex-girlfriend. When principal Shannon Sharpe confronts him and asks him to stay away from the school, the spark between

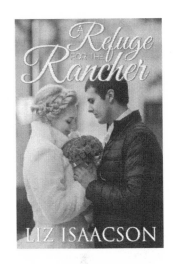

them is instant and hot. Shannon's expecting a transfer very soon, but she also needs a summer outdoor coordinator—and Grant fits the bill. Just because he's handsome and everything Shannon's ever wanted in a cowboy husband means nothing. Will Grant and Shannon be able to survive the summer or will the Utah heat be too much for them to handle?

A Marriage for the Marine: A Fuller Family Novel - Brush Creek Brides Romance (Book 7): Tate Benson can't believe he's come to Nowhere, Utah, to fix up a house that hasn't been inhabited in years. But he has. Because he's retired from the Marines and looking to start a life as a police officer in small-town Brush Creek. Wren Fuller has her hands full most days running her family's company. When Tate calls and demands a maid for that morning, she decides to have the calls forwarded to her cell and go help him out. She didn't know he was moving in next door, and she's completely unprepared for his handsomeness, his kind heart, and his wounded soul.Can Tate and Wren weather a relationship when they're also next-door neighbors?

A Fiancé for the Firefighter: A Fuller Family Novel - Brush Creek Brides Romance (Book 8): Cora Wesley comes to Brush Creek, hoping to get some in-the-wild firefighting training as she prepares to put in her application to be a hotshot. When she meets Brennan Fuller, the spark between them is hot and instant. As they get to know

each other, her deadline is constantly looming over them, and Brennan starts to wonder if he can break ranks in the family business. He's okay mowing lawns and hanging out with his brothers, but he dreams of being able to go to college and become a landscape architect, but he's just not sure it can be done. Will Cora and Brennan be able to endure their trials to find true love?

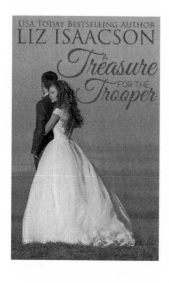

A Treasure for the Trooper: A Fuller Family Novel - Brush Creek Brides Romance (Book 9): Dawn Fuller has made some mistakes in her life, and she's not proud of the way McDermott Boyd found her off the road one day last year. She's spent a hard year wrestling with her choices and trying to fix them, glad for McDermott's acceptance and friendship. He lost his wife years ago, done his best with his daughter, and now he's ready to move on. Can McDermott help Dawn find a way past her former mistakes and down a path that leads to love, family, and happiness?

A Date for the Detective: A Fuller Family Novel - Brush Creek Brides Romance (Book 10): Dahlia Reid is one of the best detectives Brush Creek and the surrounding towns has ever had. She's given up on the idea of marriage—and pleasing her mother—and has dedicated herself fully to her job. Which is great, since one of the most perplexing cases of her career  has come to town. Kyler Fuller thinks he's finally ready to move past the woman who ghosted him years ago. He's cut his hair, and he's ready to start dating. Too bad every woman he's been out with is about as interesting as a lamppost—until Dahlia. He finds her beautiful, her quick wit a breath of fresh air, and her intelligence sexy. Can Kyler and Dahlia use their faith to find a way through the obstacles threatening to keep them apart?

A Partner for the Paramedic: A Fuller Family Novel - Brush Creek Brides Romance (Book 11): Jazzy Fuller has always been overshadowed by her prettier, more popular twin, Fabiana. Fabi meets paramedic Max Robinson at the park and sets a date with him only to come down with the flu. So she convinces Jazzy to cut her hair and take her place on the date. And the spark between Jazzy and Max is hot and instant...if only he knew she wasn't her sister, Fabi.

Max drives the ambulance for the town of Brush Creek with is partner Ed Moon, and neither of them have been all that lucky in love. Until Max suggests to who he thinks is Fabi that they should double with Ed and Jazzy. They do, and Fabi is smitten with the steady, strong Ed Moon. As each twin falls further and further in love with their respective paramedic, it becomes obvious they'll need to come clean about the switcheroo sooner rather than later...or risk losing their hearts.

A Catch for the Chief: A Fuller Family Novel - Brush Creek Brides Romance (Book 12): Berlin Fuller has struck out with the dating scene in Brush Creek more times than she cares to admit. When she makes a deal with her friends that they can choose the next man she goes out with, she didn't dream they'd pick surly Cole Fairbanks, the new Chief of Police.

His friends call him the Beast and challenge him to complete ten dates that summer or give up his bonus check. When Berlin approaches him, stuttering about the deal with her friends and claiming they don't actually have to go out, he's intrigued. As the summer passes, Cole finds himself burning both ends of the candle to keep up with his job and his new relationship. When he unleashes the Beast one time too many, Berlin will have to decide if she can tame him or if she should walk away.

ABOUT LIZ

Liz Isaacson writes inspirational romance, usually set in Texas, or Montana, or anywhere else horses and cowboys exist. She lives in Utah, where she teaches elementary school, taxis her daughter to dance several times a week, and eats a lot of Ferrero Rocher while writing. Find her on her website at lizisaacson.com.

Made in the USA
Columbia, SC
20 March 2020